UNTIL WE FLY

The Beautifully Broken Series
Book Four

By Courtney Cole

Sometimes…before we fall, we fly

Lakehouse Press, Inc.

This book is an original publication of Lakehouse Press, Inc.
All rights reserved.

Copyright © 2014, Courtney Cole
Cover Design by The Cover Lure (Matthew Phillips)

Library of Congress Cataloging-in-publication data

Cole, Courtney
        Until We Fly/Courtney Cole/Lakehouse Press Inc/Trade pbk
ed

ISBN 13: **978-0692255629**
ISNB 10: **0692255621**

Printed in the United States of America

Dedication

For hearts that are aching, for souls that are broken.

Fluctuat nec mergitur
(She is tossed by the waves, but she does not sink)

Choose not to sink.

Prologue

I'm dreaming of bullets and blood. Like always.

There are the screams, of course, because there are always screams. High-pitched and shrill, low and keening. They're full of pain, full of anguish, full of torment. It's a torturous sound and I twist and turn, trying to get away from it.

That's when I realize something.

Outside of my dream, out where the silence is thick and heavy, there's a sound.

A real sound.

The ring of a phone is breaking the silence apart, splintering the night into a million pieces. My eyes snap open, staring blearily at the clock.

Three a.m.

A call at this hour is never anything good.

Old training kicks in and my senses numb, detaching me from the situation as I fumble for my phone. Whatever it is, I'll be calm and ready. That's who I am and what I'm trained to be.

Punching a button, I hold the device to my ear. I wait, expecting to hear my best friend, Gabe, his sister Jacey, or any number of our friends. I'm always the go-to person to bail someone out of trouble, mostly because I *am* calm and unflustered. I don't judge people for their shit. For these reasons, I'm used to these calls.

But I'm not used to the voice who speaks in the darkness.

A thin, frail voice I haven't heard in years.

"Brand?"

The voice is like a punch to my gut and I'm instantly still, every nerve ending frozen.

"Mom," I utter, the word foreign on my tongue.

She doesn't acknowledge that I even spoke. She sighs, a shaky sound in the dark.

"It's your dad. He had a heart attack tonight."

She pauses and I say nothing, although my heart begins to pound, filling my ears with a rush, rush, rushing sound. My blood is ice being pumped through my veins, chilling my fingers and my toes, deadening every emotion.

I don't answer her.

A silent beat passes.

Then another.

When she speaks again, her voice is tired and rough.

"He's gone, Brand."

I remain silent and frozen, unable to move, although my palms immediately grow sweaty, my breath rapid in my throat. I'm afraid if I speak, this won't be real. It will be part of my dream, and when I wake, it will all go away.

So I don't say a word.

Be real.

"I need you to come home," my mother adds.

Her call to action frees me and I'm able to move again. I nod, once, curtly.

"I'll be there."

Because this is real.

I hang up without another word, my hands shaky.

I stare at my left hand, at my fingers, thick and long. I'm a grown man. Yet the mere thought of my father instinctively causes my hands to shake, like the scared boy I once was. I allow myself to feel the impotent emotion for only one moment, before I channel the fear into rage, a blinding hot rage that I have every right to feel.

My father is dead.

5

I should be upset, devastated even. A normal person would be.

But in addition to my rage, there's only one thing I feel.

Relief.

Chapter One

Nora

"Nora, are you listening?"

No.

I turn my attention away from the cars driving slowly by on the small town's Main Street to look at my father. Maxwell Greene's piercing eyes are trained on me now, the silver at his temples glinting in the sun, and I gulp.

"Yes, of course," I lie.

He nods, pacified.

"Good. I know this last year of law school was difficult, but it's over now. I want you to take the summer off, rest here in Angel Bay with your mother, then in the Fall, you'll take over the legal team at Green Corp as planned."

He's ecstatic, of course, because it's everything he's ever wanted. It's always been the plan, since the moment I started elementary school. Probably, actually, since before I was born.

"What about Peter?" I ask him hesitantly, picturing the middle-aged attorney who until now has been the Vice President of Legal Affairs for our company. He's always been nice to me, always showed me pictures of his pretty wife and four daughters.

My father rolls his eyes. "He'll be cut loose. He's known this was coming for a while, I'm sure. Everyone knew you were at Stanford studying law. They can connect dots, Nora."

He's so blasé about ruining someone's life. I swallow hard, fiddling with the straw in my glass of lemonade. The umbrella from our little bistro table on the wide sidewalk casts a shadow across my shoulders, and I almost shiver. I'm not sure if it's from the chilly lake breeze, or if it's from my father's cold attitude.

He stares harshly at me now.

"Nora, you've got to grow a set of balls. There's no pussy-footing around corporate law. You have to kill or be killed. I need you to be a Greene and do what it takes. *Be who I need you to be.*"

His voice is even colder than his stare. I shirk away from it out of old habit.

"Okay," I whisper.

My mother pipes up finally, from across the table, smiling a magnificent smile. Out of all of us, she's always been the kindest. The sweetest. And she knows I need rescuing right now. I see it in her soft blue eyes.

"Ma belle fille," she sings, reaching over and grasping my hand. "We'll have a glorious summer. You can ride Rebel, you can rest on the beach, we'll get manicures and pedicures... we'll have tea and croissants. It will be lovely. You need the rest."

My beautiful daughter. My mother's French accent is as strong as ever, even though she's lived in the states since she married my father twenty-five years ago. It charms everyone who hears it.

I smile at her, genuine now.

"Thanks, maman. I'm looking forward to spending time with you. I've missed you."

That's not a lie.

What I haven't missed is my father. And the constant lectures about being "a good Greene" and how I need to do what I can for the greater good of the family and our business.

No matter the personal cost.

And my personal cost has been great.

Not that anyone cares.

But the bitterness is welling up again and if I don't tamp it down, it will overwhelm me. That won't help anything.

She doesn't know, I remind myself.

"How's Rebel?" I ask my mother, purposely changing the subject to that of my old horse. I haven't seen him since last summer. My mom chatters about him, about how fat he's getting and I turn away again.

To make my resentment recede, I look at the clouds, at the cars, at the quaint little shops, at the intersection. Anything to distract me, anything to make the bitter taste of what happened to me go away.

She doesn't know.

But my father does. I glance at him, and the anger rears its head again. Yes, he knows. *Do what it takes, Nora.*

I grit my teeth. It's over now. It's over. No one can fix it anyway. All I can do now is be a good Greene.

With a hard stare, I focus on the intersection again, willing myself to find interest in something else.

Anything else.

A red car comes to a stop, then goes through. Angel Bay is so small that there's only one major intersection and it's right here in front of the cafe. There's not even a light, just a four-way stop.

If you want to people watch, this is the best place to do it.

My mother chats in her charming voice, and I absently stare as a white suburban turns left. A yellow Beetle then lets a young mother pushing a stroller cross the street before he goes. He waves as he passes, a friendly stranger.

I smile. Angel Bay is full of friendly strangers. They're used to summer tourists, and they're friendly to each of them, happy to have their tourist dollars, happy to share their little town by Lake Michigan.

Down the road, a faded white bus coasts down the road. Signs are fastened to the sides and I can just make one out.

Honk for the Annual Troop 52 Camping Trip.

I smile again at the little cub scouts who have their faces pressed to the windows. They're probably headed for Warren Dunes State Park... so they're almost there, and as little boys often are, they're getting antsy.

Behind the bus, a huge navy blue pick-up truck follows at a respectable distance. The windows are tinted, but I see a glimpse of sunny blonde hair. I stare a bit harder, out of idle curiosity. People watching has always been a hobby. Watching other people's lives distracts me from my own.

It's pathetic, but true.

As the truck draws closer and I get a better view of the driver's face, I almost gasp aloud.

It can't be.

I peer closer, my eyes narrowed behind my sunglasses. The driver of the truck is also wearing sunglasses, which makes it harder to see for sure.

But that blond hair... honey blond hair that it looks like it has been kissed by the sun. The chiseled cheekbones, cleft in the chin, the strong jawline, the proud nose. I would recognize that profile anywhere, even through a heavily tinted windshield, even though the last time I'd seen it was almost ten years ago.

Brand Killien.

No way.

I realize that I'm holding my breath and I inhale, still staring at him.

He still looks like a Norse god, still like the boy I had fallen in love with so many years ago. He didn't know, of course, because I'm four years younger. I was *so* not on his radar. But he was always on mine...for a couple of reasons.

One, because he's always been the most beautiful thing I've ever seen.

Two, and even more importantly, he makes me feel good. Safe and sound. Like when I'm with him, nothing can hurt me, nothing can touch me.

I fantasized about him every single summer, and then one year, I came back to Angel Bay after a long winter, only to find that Brand wasn't here. He'd gone away to college and then joined the Army.

Every summer after that, I watched for him to come home.

Every summer after that, he wasn't here.

People chattered, of course, because Angel Bay is so small and that's what small town people do. In the tiny grocery, I heard that he became some badass special ops soldier, that he was in the Rangers in Afghanistan. In the café, I heard that something terrible happened to him there, that he'd come home after that.

But much to my disappointment, he never came back to Angel Bay.

Until now.

Butterflies explode in my stomach, their wings tickling my ribs, their writhing velvety bodies pressed against my diaphragm, making it hard to breathe. It's like even they know the reverence of this moment, the absolute miracle that it is.

Brand Killien is here.

A farm truck pulling a flat-bed trailer lurches forward at the intersection, blocking my view momentarily. I lean forward, trying to subtly find Brand again, just to make sure he's there, that I hadn't just imagined him.

That's when I see the problem, and even though it happens too quickly for me to even scream, it seems to happen in slow motion at the same time.

A dump truck barrels through the intersection from the other side, slamming into the ammonia tank on the farm truck's trailer.

The explosion is immediate and severe.

I feel the intense rush of heat before I hear the boom. But when the boom comes, it splits apart the sky. It's so loud that it reverberates in my chest, rattling each of my ribs and setting the butterflies free. Suddenly, I'm in the air. My legs dangle like a pitiful rag doll and the breeze is all around me. *I'm in the breeze. I* am *the breeze.*

Things come in visceral snippets now as I fly.

Heat.

Noise.

Screams.

Cracks.

Glass.

My flight is short and I slam into something hard, my head cracking against the floor. The floor?

Blackness.

Heat.

When I open my eyes, I'm not sure how much time has passed, only that my head feels heavy, a splitting pain coming from the back of it. With shaking fingers, I touch it, and my fingertips come back covered in blood.

I look up.

The heat is from fire. And the fire is all around.

I'm in a pile of rubble in what used to be the café. Boards and ceiling and tables are piled around me, and people are on the floor. Dust is everywhere and I can hardly see through it. But I can see the fire.

And I can see Brand.

Like some sort of magnificent and fierce angel, he strides through the dark smoke, and I see him pry the school bus doors open. He leaps inside, and a scant moment later, he emerges with a child in his muscled arms. He hands the child to someone, then goes back into the smoking, charred bus. Over and over, I watch this process.

Some of the children he carries out are bloody, some are limp. But he continues to make the trips.

Finally, he comes out empty handed.

He stands still for a moment, and I see how his shirt is ripped down the front. I can see a chiseled washboard behind the large tear. I see how soot is smeared across his cheeks, and the same soot has turned his hair black.

I see him take a deep breath, I see him look around at the carnage on the street, looking for someone else to save.

And then he sees me.

I *do* need saved. More than he'll ever know.

His eyes are a blue so bright that I can't even name it. Sapphire, maybe? They shine through the soot, through the flames. He focuses on me, then with long steps, he comes to me. Straight to me. Through the chaos, through the havoc.

"Miss, are you alright?" his voice is husky, probably from the smoke. I can't move.

"I'm stuck," I manage to tell him. "My legs."

My legs are beneath splintered boards, boards that used to be a café wall. As I glance up at Brand, I see my parents on the street, standing with an EMT. I can see my mother's frantic arm movements, and I can read her lips.

My daughter.

I take a breath, but there's no way she'd hear me if I called. She'll have to wait.

Brand draws my attention back to him, back to his brilliant blue eyes, by speaking.

"I'm going to get this stuff off of you. I'll try not to hurt you," he tells me calmly. With muscular arms, he lifts the jagged boards off of me, one by one. True to his word, he doesn't hurt me.

When he's finished, when I'm free, he doesn't help me stand.

He bends and scoops me up instead.

My head rests against his chest and I can hear his heart as he carries me effortlessly through the mayhem.

Ba-bump.

Ba-bump.

His heart is as strong as he is.

I focus on that, on the strong beats, instead of looking at the people on the floor. Instead of looking at the blood, or smelling the smoke, or having a panic attack.

"Are you okay?" Brand asks me, looking down at me. His face is confident, his voice calm. "You're going to be all right."

I nod because I believe him, because how could I not trust a voice that sure of itself?

But then it doesn't matter.

Because out of nowhere, I hear a nauseatingly loud crack, and all of a sudden, the wall next to us comes down in a mass of metallic shrieks and groans and shards.

 It shears my arm, and I can smell the blood.

I'm knocked free from Brand's safe grasp, yanked from his arms, and I'm falling, falling, falling.

Then it all goes black and stays that way.

Chapter Two

Brand

Fucking son-of-a-bitch.

White hot pain rips through me, from my hip to my ankle. I grimace, trying to pull myself out of the wreckage, to no avail. I'm the one who is s5tuck now, firmly and painfully in a mountain of broken wood and cinder.

The smoke surrounding me brings back instant memories of Afghanistan, of bombs and blood. But I shake those images away. I'm not there. I'm here. And I've got to keep my wits.

The girl.

The girl I was carrying, the girl with the dark red hair and big blue eyes. She trusted me. I saw it on her face.

I twist to find her, scanning everything around me. And then I see her thin arm, sticking out of a pile of rubble. I know it's hers because of the turquoise bracelet on her small wrist.

"Help!" I call out to the EMTs who are now on the scene. One hears me, and rushes my way, but I wave him toward the girl.

"Get her first!" I tell him. "She's under that shit. Get her first. It's crushing her."

He does as I ask, and it takes two of them to dig her out. I watch them carry her out, I watch how her eyes are still closed, I watch them stretch her limp body onto a waiting gurney before they come back for me.

Fuck.

"Thank you," I tell them sincerely. They gingerly move the wood and the drywall and the twisted metal that is holding me down, before they roll me onto a stretcher.

"I'm fine," I try and tell them, as I attempt to get up.

But I can't get up. My left leg is twisted beneath me, my foot turned an unnatural way. I stare at it, aghast and astonished, noticing the way my knee is turned out, while my ankle is turned in.

Fuck.

I don't feel the pain, so I know I'm in shock. I drop back against the stretcher, as they wheel me toward a waiting ambulance.

My leg was shattered in Afghanistan. I had multiple surgeries, months of physical therapy and I was only just starting to walk without a limp. And for what? *To have it annihilated again?* Here in fucking Angel Bay?

Fucking hell.

They load me up and close the door and I stare at the white metal for a second before I close my eyes. This can't be happening. This isn't real.

But it's real.

The sirens, loud and wailing, tell me that.

Numbly, I wait. Then something occurs to me. *Why are they using the siren for a broken leg?*

I barely have the thought before my fingers grow cold, and my thoughts begin to get fuzzy, muddled.

What the hell?

But then it doesn't matter, because I'm so fucking tired. Nothing matters, not the pain, or the lack of it, or even the girl.

My arms and legs grow heavy and I close my eyes, a sigh rattling my ribcage.

The girl. Her blue eyes are the last things I see before I close my eyes.

It seems like only minutes before the ambulance shrieks to a stop and I'm being bustled out.

I grab one of the EMTs arms as they race me into the hospital.

"What's wrong?"

He stares down at me as he runs. "Don't worry. They'll fix you."

I fall back onto the gurney and all I can do is watch everything happening. Waves of utter exhaustion and sleepiness pass through me and all I want to do is close my eyes.

So I do, but I can't sleep because some damn faceless person keeps asking me questions, all the while other faceless people prod at my leg and cut off my pants.

What's your name?

"Brand Killien," I mutter.

How old are you?

"Twenty-seven."

Are you allergic to anything?

No.

Can we call anyone for you?

"No."

I open my eyes when they jam an IV into my arm, and the lights are bright, and the medicine feeding into me blurs it all together.

A nurse's face blurs in front of me.

"You're going in to surgery, sweetheart," she tells me. I can't see her face even though my eyes are wide open. "Your artery was nicked. They have to fix it."

My fucking artery was nicked?

You've got to be kidding me. *I survived the bloody hills of Afghanistan. I'm not going to bleed to death here. No fucking way. Holy shit. Why didn't I have them call Gabe or Jacey... just in case?*

I try to mutter that, to tell them to call Gabe, but they can't understand me.

Another face blurs over me, someone with black hair. "Everything will be all right, sir. Just count backward from one hundred."

The light swirls, the noise echoes.

Ninety-Nine.

Ninety-Eight.

Ninety-Seven.

Nothing.

Nothing.

I hear my father's heavy footsteps stepping out of my little sister's room, closing the door with a click, then leaning heavily on the bannister as he walks down the stairs.

Seventeen-Creak.

Sixteen-Creak.

Each of the seventeen steps groans, and then there is silence once again. Staring up at the ceiling, I wait until I hear the muffler of his old truck fire up before I breathe again.

He's gone.

Relief rushes through me and I feel stupid. I'm six years old. I shouldn't be so afraid.

But I am.

I get up to go to the bathroom, something I'd never do when he was still at home. I wouldn't risk it. I tip-toe into the kitchen and grab a handful of cookies, being careful not to tip over the cookie jar onto the floor, before I make my way back to my room, running through the shadows, leaping into bed.

I turn onto my side and stare out my windows as I chew the chocolate chips. My mother had made them tonight, specially for dinner, only my father wouldn't let me have one.

"Boys who don't watch their little sisters don't get cookies," he'd told me sternly, eyeing me with his cold blue eyes.

I'd gulp and peered through my eyelashes at Alison. She was happily munching on a cookie, the crumbs gathering on the front of her shirt. Her grubby fingers grasped her sugary treasure and she was oblivious to the trouble I'm in because of her.

"But I was watching her," I told my father. "I tried to make her come in and wash up for dinner, she just wouldn't listen."

My father was unsympathetic. "She's only four. You have to look out for her. You're bigger than she is. Are you telling me that you can't take ahold of her arm and bring her in? Are you that weak, Branden?"

I gulped, shaking my head. "No."

He shook his head, his steely eyes piercing me. "I'm not sure about that. If it happens again, I'll have to teach you a lesson. I'll show you exactly how you can make someone smaller and weaker do what you want."

Panic welled up in me then, and it wells up in me now, at the mere memory.

I don't want to get that lesson.

I stare out the window at the lake, watching the water roll gently into the beach. At night, the sand looks silver. The gulls are asleep, so everything is silent but for the rippling water.

A white ball appears, floating to and fro in the tide, and I watch it for a while, watching as it floats, then disappears.

I wish I could be that ball and float far from here.

With a start, I open my eyes and the light is blinding. I squint my eyes toward it, trying to process where I am. Medicinal smells, sterile walls.

The hospital.

I groan, and my throat is raspy. I recognize that feeling. I must've had a breathing tube. Surgery. I also recognize the foggy aftereffects of anesthesia.

What the hell?

A nurse bustles through the door, her eyes widening when she sees me awake. Her cool fingers find my pulse, counting the beats.

"Mr. Killien," she smiles. "I'm so glad you're awake. How are you feeling?"

I swallow again, trying to swallow past the raw throat.

"I don't know," I tell her honestly. "What happened?"

Her eyes are full of sympathy.

"You saved a bus full of kids," she tells me. "There was an accident, a truck ran a stop-sign and slammed into an ammonia tank. There was an explosion. Do you remember?"

I think on that, and I do remember. I remember the smoke and the blood and the kids.

And then I remember the red-haired girl.

"There was a girl," I tell the nurse. "A woman, I mean. Red hair. I was carrying her when the building collapsed on us. Is she okay? Did she live?"

God, she had to live. She trusted me. Her eyes, so big and blue, told me that. She counted on me to carry her out and I didn't.

My gut squeezes and I wince in pain.

But the nurse is already nodding. "Everyone lived, Mr. Killien. And I think you mean Ms. Greene. She's here and she's been asking about you, too. Can I tell her that you're awake? She's been very worried about you."

Ms. Greene?

I nod and the nurse smiles.

"I'll tell her. She's been waiting here for the last several hours. She was lucky- She and her parents only sustained minor injuries. She didn't want to leave until you woke up."

I sigh with relief. Even though I couldn't carry her out, she's okay.

Thank God.

I close my eyes, my mind fuzzy from anesthesia. The room spins outside of my eyelids, but inside of them, it's black and still.

And then someone clears her voice softly.

I open my eyes.

They instantly meet the blue-eyed gaze of the girl.

Ms. Greene.

For a second, there's something familiar there, something that niggles at me. Do I know her?

But I scan the rest of her... the long dark red hair that flows halfway down her back, her slender body, her lush chest and hips. Even through the fog of medicine, my groin registers her obvious beauty.

I'd remember if I knew her.

She smiles, a brilliant white smile. I notice she has dirt on her cheeks and forehead.

"Are you okay?" she asks, her voice as soft as silk.

I nod. "Yeah. I will be, I guess."

She looks at my leg sympathetically, her eyes clouded. "I'm so sorry. You wouldn't even have been in the café if it weren't for me. It's my fault you're here in this bed."

I'm already shaking my head. No way. I know what it's like to take responsibility for something that wasn't my fault. I won't let this girl do it.

"No," I tell her firmly. "I wanted to help. If I hadn't seen you, I'd have seen someone else, so I would've been in there anyway."

Probably.

She shakes her head slightly, the edges of her mouth tilted up.

"Such a gentleman," she murmurs. She slides into the chair by my bed, graceful and elegant.

"You don't recognize me, do you, Brand?"

My head snaps up when she uses my name.

She does know me.

I examine her again. Her face. Her nose. Her hair. Her eyes.

Ms. Greene.

The Greenes.

Good lord.

I fight a groan. I've been gone from here too long. I've forgotten too many things. In this case, the Greenes are an Angel Bay staple. They own a huge lakeside estate that they only reside at in the summers, and they're members at the country club where I used to work.

I do know her. Or, I remember the girl she used to be. She's certainly grown up now.

"I used to park your father's car at the club," I say slowly.

Nora smiles. "And you picked me up out of the dirt once. Do you remember that?"

I do.

Nora was younger, a teenager then, and her horse had thrown her off. I'd been walking to the clubhouse to get a soda for my break and I'd seen the whole thing. She'd gone sprawling into the dirt, and the first thing she'd done was stare furtively around, to make sure no one had seen.

It was a nasty spill though, so I had gone to check on her. Her hands were shaky and I didn't want to leave her alone, even though it was strictly against the rules for valet staff to mingle with club members.

"Did my father see?" she'd asked me quickly, her lip caught in her teeth. There was a spot of blood from her braces, and I'd reached out and wiped it off for her. She wasn't concerned about her cut lip, though. She was terrified that her father had seen her mistake.

"No," I assured her. "I'm the only one around."

"Thank God," she'd breathed.

"Do you want me to go get him?" I asked her quickly, thinking that he might help her calm down.

She'd grabbed my arm, hard, her fingernails sinking in. "Please don't," she'd begged, her eyes suddenly full of tears. "Please."

It had shocked me, her immediate and adamant refusal. It was like she was scared of him. I'd assured her that I wouldn't get him, and I'd taken her inside to calm her down myself. I stayed with her for half an hour.

"I got written up for that," I remember slowly. Nora's face clouds over.

"You did?" she asks in confusion. "Why in the world?"

From the astonished expression on her face, I almost believe that she doesn't know.

"Your dad complained," I tell her simply. "Someone mentioned it to him, and he reported me. Valets weren't supposed to socialize with members, you know."

"You weren't socializing," she points out. "You were helping me."

I shrug. "It was a long time ago."

But her eyes are still dismayed. A part of me finds satisfaction in that. Maybe she's not the ice bitch I expected her to be. With a father like hers, though, I don't know how that's possible.

"I just wanted to check on you," Nora tells me now hesitantly. "I feel responsible and I wanted to help. So I told them they might want to call your mother. You didn't have any contacts listed in your wallet, and your phone was password protected."

My mother? I stopped listening to her words as soon as she mentioned my mother.

"Why would they call my mother?" I ask stupidly. Nora shakes her head in confusion.

"Because you were here alone. I didn't know who else to call. I thought you might want a family member..." her voice trails off as she stares at my face. "I see now that I was wrong. I'm so sorry. I was just trying to help."

She was. I'm sure of that.

But calling my mother was the furthest possible thing from helping.

"Did she even bother to come?" I ask tiredly. I'd driven twelve hours to get here because she summoned me, and I doubt my mother even bothered to come to the hospital.

Nora shakes her head hesitantly. "She told the nurse that she'd come pick you up when you were released."

Yet I'd gone into surgery with a nicked artery. For all she knew, I could've died on the table and she still didn't come.

Why does that surprise me? She didn't bother to call and check on me when I was on the battlefields in Afghanistan, either.

Nausea rolls through my stomach and I swallow hard.

"Well, that's not a surprise. Thank you for trying to help, Ms. Greene. I appreciate it. I know you must be tired. You don't need to stay with me."

She lifts her blue eyes. "Call me Nora."

I nod. "Okay. Thanks for checking on me, Nora. I'm glad you're all right."

Her eyes soften, glistening with something I can't name. "Thank you for *making* me okay. You pulled me out, Brand. If it weren't for you..."

I interrupt. "If I hadn't pulled you out, someone else would've."

She shrugs. "Maybe. But either way, thank you. I'm going to check on you again tomorrow."

Something soft lives in her eyes, but then she hides it. I should tell her not to come, I should tell her to not even bother. But the soft look in her eyes, that fleeting expression, kills the words on my tongue. She seems like a person who doesn't let that softness shine through often.

Instead, I nod. "I'm sure I'll still be here."

I glance down at my leg and sigh heavily. Nora almost flinches.

"I hope you get some rest," she says as she walks out. "I'll see you tomorrow."

She walks toward the open door, and I watch her hips gently sway until she abruptly stops in the doorway. She turns and looks at me, her gaze meeting mine. Electricity jolts between us, between her soft gaze and my own.

Hers holds a promise. *I'll be back.*

For some reason, I like that. Maybe because I'm from a world where there were never any promises, where tomorrow was never expected or hoped for, where parents don't even show up at the hospital.

Whatever.

I shouldn't encourage her. I'm not going to be here for long.

So I look away, breaking our gaze.

I know she walks away because I can feel the absence of her stare. I glance back, and sure enough, she's gone.

Oddly, I feel alone now.

I don't really even know her, but now that she's gone, I feel alone.

I'm not alone for long.

A doctor enters my room after a few minutes.

"Mr. Killien," he says, flipping through my chart. "You were really lucky today. Your artery was nicked, but we repaired it. Your leg, however… " he trails off, then refocuses. "Your leg was obviously previously injured, probably severely. You had several plates and screws from your foot to your hip. You hyper-extended your knee today, but you also re-damaged the soft-tissue around your ankle. I know you're probably tired of physical therapy, but it's going to take some diligent PT to strengthen that area again. I'm sorry."

His voice really is sorry and so are his eyes, but that doesn't make his news any less grim.

"Your thigh needs absolute rest. I don't want you to break open those sutures. And your knee... stay off of it for now, no weight bearing. You can bear weight as tolerated as time goes by. Did you injure your leg overseas?" he asks. I look at him questioningly. He glances down.

"Your tattoos. I assume you're a soldier. Or you were."

I nod once. "Yeah. My HUMVEE exploded. My leg was shattered. It took months of rehab for me to walk."

The doctor nods grimly. "I thought as much. I don't know what to tell you for a prognosis this time. Since your previous injury was so severe, it's going to make recovering this time a bit harder. I have no doubt that you'll overcome it, you'll just have to be very diligent with rehab. Rest it, ice it, stay off of it."

His words are meant to bolster me, but they don't.

Instead, I close my eyes.

"We'll send a physical therapist to your house. Where will you be staying?"

That's a good question.

"I'll probably be going back home," I tell him quickly. But he shakes his head.

"I don't want you to go anywhere for at least a week or two. Primarily, I don't want your artery disturbed. We patched it up, but as you might be aware, femoral artery injuries are nothing to mess with. I don't want you jarring it with travel. But also, you've got to keep weight off that foot. Your driver's license listed a Connecticut address. Is that where you live?"

I nod. "My father just died. I'm only here to take care of that. I'll be going home soon."

The doctor is already shaking his head. "I would rest here for at least a couple of weeks. If possible, you should stay longer, to get that knee healed up. If you absolutely can't, then you can travel when your artery completely heals. Until then, though, you've got to stay put."

He goes over a few other things with me, and then he slips back out. I do the only thing I can think of.

I call Gabe.

As my best friend and business partner, he and I have been through hell and high water together. We spent every summer together while he was staying here with his grandparents, we attended West Point together, we made the Rangers together, and we were together when our HUMVEE was bombed by Taliban rebels.

He answers on the first ring.

"Whattup, bro?"

I quickly give him a run down.

"Jesus," Gabe breathes. "I'm sorry, Brand. I had no idea. I'll be on the next flight."

"No," I tell him quickly. "There's no reason to do that. It's just a leg injury, not heart surgery. You can't make me heal quicker. But can I use your cottage?"

Gabe and his sister Jacey had inherited their grandparents' lake cottage. I spent so much time down there with them growing up that honestly, it feels like a second home.

Gabe doesn't hesitate. He doesn't ask about my mother, he doesn't ask any questions at all. He simply agrees.

"Of course," he tells me. "Mi casa is su casa. You know where we keep the key. But when I tell Jacey, she's going to freak out. She's in Europe with Dominic for a couple of weeks, but I bet she'll be on the first plane home when I tell her."

Gabe's sister. Beautiful, feisty, blonde Jacey. She was like a little sister to me, until all of a sudden, she wasn't. Hormones and sex appeal suck balls.

I hesitate, and Gabe knows why. I'd fallen in love with Jacey, and she'd married someone else. It was a bitter pill.

"Dude," he tells me. "She loves you. She's going to want to come mother you."

Dude. She didn't love me *enough*.

But I don't say that. I also don't say that I can't bear for her to come smother me with attention.... Attention which is only that of someone who considers me 'like a brother.' I can't fucking take it.

"Then let's not tell her for a week or two," I suggest. "She's in Europe, for God's sake. Let's not spoil her trip."

Gabe sighs. "Fine. But you get to be the one to explain why we didn't call right away."

"Fine," I mutter.

"Don't worry about work," Gabe tells me. "You know it's practically taking care of itself right now anyway. Can I set up some sort of home nurse or something? You're not going to be able to travel home for a while, dude."

I sigh.

"I know." The anesthesia has worn off enough that hot fingers of pain are beginning to wrap around my knee and ankle. By tomorrow, it's going to hurt like hell. "No. I don't want a home nurse. Thank you, though."

"Let me know if you change your mind," Gabe tells me. "And if you decide you need me, call me. I'll be on the next plane."

"Stay home with your wife," I tell him. "I've got this."

"I know you do."

Gabe hangs up and I stare at the wall.

Fuck this. I didn't want to be here in the first place, and now I'm fucking stuck here.

I can't roll onto my side, I can't even get up to take a piss.

Growling, I stuff the crinkly hospital pillow over my head to drown out the hospital sounds.

This is real.

I need to get used to it.

Chapter Three

Nora

I stare at the little newspaper on the kitchen island.

Brand's picture is plastered to the front, along with a big headline.

Local Hero Hasn't Lost His Touch.

The story goes on to detail how Brand was a Lt. Colonel in the Seventy-Fifth Regiment Army Rangers, served a colorful stint overseas in Afghanistan and earned a Purple Heart. His father died last week and Lt. Col Killien retuned home only to save a bus of cub scouts upon arrival here.

The picture was taken by a by-stander, and it shows Brand carrying a kid off the smoking bus. There's fire all around him, but he doesn't even seem to notice. Instead, he's tall and strong, and rises out of the wreckage like the hero he is.

He's here because his father died.

I don't even realize I have goose-bumps until my mother sits next to me and rubs them off of my arms.

"That was something, wasn't it?" she murmurs, handing me a glass of fresh orange juice as she glances at the picture of Brand.

"It was something," I agree. "He saved me, maman. He picked me up and carried me out of that building."

"Well, almost," my mother smiles. "But he was certainly amazing and I, for one, am certainly in his debt for coming to your rescue. Isn't that the boy who used to work at the club? I seem to remember that you were frequently tongue-tied whenever he was around."

I roll my eyes.

"I'm all grown up now," I announce. "No one tongue ties me."

Well, hardly anyone. But that's neither here nor there.

"I'm going to the hospital again today," I tell her. "Do you need anything from town? When is dad going back to Chicago?"

Mom looks away. "He left early this morning, my love."

Without bothering to say goodbye, or make sure that I'm really okay. I shake my head. It's for the best. I didn't want to see him anyway.

I push away from the counter and kiss my mother's cheek, grabbing the newspaper. "I'll be home later."

My mother perks up and smiles at me. "Rebel is waiting for you," she says brightly. "You'd better take him some carrots on your way out."

Of course I will. The mere thought of my old horse always brightens me up. I've had him since I was a kid, and although he's getting old, he's still perfectly capable of leisurely strolls on the beach. I head straight down to the stables, only stopping to say hello to Julian. The groundskeeper/groomsman has been with our family since before I was born. He takes care of this house all winter while we're gone.

"Miss Nora," he beams, holding his tanned arms out. I fold into him and inhale. Julian always smells like sunshine and happiness. "I've been waiting for you. Rebel too. He isn't the same when you're away."

I laugh as I take a step back. "He should be used to it. I've been away at school for six years."

Julian grins back. "Yes, but you come back every summer. He waits for that all year."

31

A sad but true fact: Rebel was my best friend growing up. My father never approved of any friends I tried to bring home from school, so I never had a proverbial BFF. Rebel was a poor substitution, but he did his best.

"It's because I bring him carrots," I announce, holding out the orange veggies. "You starve him when I'm gone."

Julian chuckles, rolling his dark eyes. "Yeah, he's neglected. I think he's fat enough to roll out of the stables now."

I giggle, and continue on my way, anxious to see my old pet.

Rebel nickers when he sees me, stretching his long chestnut neck out so he can nuzzle my fingers.

"You know I come bearing gifts, don't you boy?" I murmur, stroking his silky coat. He chomps on his carrots, then nudges my hand for more.

"Nope, that's it. Julian wasn't kidding," I tell him, eyeing Rebel's barrel sized belly. "You're getting fat."

Rebel flicks his ear, regarding my comment with disdain. I giggle. "I'll come back later and ride you."

He snorts, and I wander out of the stable, and down the winding trail to the beach below. The smells here assail me... the sand, the sun, the water. It brings back instant memories of playing out here with my older brother Nate. Fun, lighthearted memories.

The images of my brother laughing and running make me smile, until they're replaced by more recent memories... of a serious, subdued Nate. The Nate who is being groomed to take over for my father. Distinguished and polished, self-disciplined and sharp.

A good Greene.

I swallow hard as I stand staring out across the water, my feet sinking into the wet sand. I pull off my sandals and dangle them in my fingers.

Tilting my face to the sun, I absorb it, soaking it in. The sun means health, and happiness and warmth. I can take all of that I can get.

What if I don't want to be a "Good Greene"? After everything that's happened this past year, I don't know if I want any of it.

But it's done now.

I start work in the Fall.

There's nothing to be done about it.

I ignore the nausea in my stomach, fighting to control the billows of anxiety that flood through me. To change the channel in my brain, I focus on something else, anything else that might distract me from my own impending fate.

The first thing that comes to me makes me smile through my panic.

A golden-haired warrior reminiscent of a Norse God.

Brand.

It's always been Brand, even if he has never known it.

All through college, even though I dated periodically, no one ever stacked up to the image of the perfect man that I held in my head, the memory that I held close to my heart, the memory that sustained me through horrible things.

Brand.

Warmth floods through me and it doesn't have anything to do with the sun.

I need to see him again.

Not just because I owe him my life, but because I *need* to see him. It's a need I can't explain, a feeling that hearkens back to my youth- and it hasn't faded over time. If possible, after yesterday, it's only flared up even stronger.

The memory of his calm face staring down at me as he carried me in his arms sends flutters through my belly.

God, he makes me feel safe.

He makes me feel safe in a world that is dangerous and ugly, a world that has only hurt me.

That's what it boils down to. No matter what ugliness has happened over this past year, there's one thing, *one person*, that can eclipse it, because in my head, he's always personified everything good in the world.

Brand can take away the ugliness and make me feel good again, even if it's only an illusion... a temporary illusion.

If I can get Brand to want me, then there must be something good in me, something redeeming, something to balance out all of the black ugliness.

I know the logic is ridiculous, but I can't help how I feel. And honestly, I'll cling to any notion that gives me hope.

And that notion is Brand.

I'm only here for the summer, and I doubt Brand will be here long, so the window of opportunity is closing by the minute. After futilely watching for him every summer, I know I can't waste this opportunity. He's only here because his father died. This might be my last chance.

I know what I have to do.

Clutching the newspaper under my arm, I drop into my car and head for the hospital.

***

I arrive just as a nurse is going over his discharge instructions.

No weight bearing at all. Keep the wounds clean and dry. Pain pills every four to six hours. Make sure you take them.

I linger in the doorway hesitantly, but then the nurse bustles by.

She smiles. "I'm glad someone is here," she told me. "He can go home today, but he can't drive himself. And...um...he doesn't have any pants."

I flush at the thought. "No pants?"

The nurse shakes her head. "No. They had to cut them off when they brought him in."

She bustles away and I look at Brand. He looks so tanned and healthy and strong in the white hospital bed, so entirely out of place in this building full of sickness.

But yet still so alone.

I can't fathom why his mother hasn't come. It makes me seethe on the inside, and I'm so terribly sorry that I called her at all. I can only imagine that she's grieving, but I'm sure Brand is too. He doesn't deserve to be alone.

As if Brand can hear my thoughts, he looks up.

He smiles when he sees me, a smile that shows off one dimple in his cheek, but doesn't quite reach his eyes. His eyes take me aback. They're beautiful, yes. They're like oceans and oceans of blue. But they're haunted by something. They scream out his demons to anyone who looks closely enough.

"Hey," he greets me. "You didn't need to come back."

Not exactly the greeting I was hoping for. I would've preferred that he was just the tiniest bit happy to see me. But I paste on a smile and pretend it doesn't matter. I'm good at that.

I toss the newspaper onto his lap.

"No? I had to come back and see the hometown hero, didn't I?"

Brand's face scrunches in confusion, but then he scans the article. "Oh, geez," he mutters. "Perfect."

That's sort of what I'm thinking as I stare at him, *perfect,* but I don't mention that, either.

"I hear you don't have any pants," I tell him instead. I try not to imagine what he looks like without pants, because, God, Nora. He's injured. In a hospital bed. Get a grip.

He grimaces. "Apparently not."

"And you can't drive," I add.

He grimaces again. "Nope."

"And I owe you. So let me take you wherever you need to go. After I get you some pants," I add quickly, red staining my cheeks.

A slow grin spreads over his face. "You don't want to walk out of here with me naked?" he asks drily.

More than you know, I think.

"Nah," I say. "We don't want to give the little old ladies heart attacks."

Or me.

"What size do you wear?" I ask, trying to put the image of Naked Brand aside.

"36x34," he answers. "But it'll be hard to put pants on, because of the knee brace. Shorts will probably be best, but you don't need to get them. I can..."

He trails off hesitantly.

"Well, I guess I do need to ask you to get them. I don't know what else I'd do. My bag's in my truck, but I don't know where my truck is."

He sounds annoyed by that, and I laugh. "I can see you don't like to depend on other people," I tell him. "I get that. But trust me, I owe you. I could buy you a million pairs of shorts and my debt wouldn't be paid. And we'll figure out where your truck is."

I walk out while he's protesting.

I return thirty minutes later with a pair of athletic shorts.

I toss them to him. "They're stretchy, so I figured they would be easier to slide on."

"That's perfect," he tells me. "I'm not fancy."

I'm awkward and hesitant, because I don't know what to do now, not while Brand holds the shorts in his hand, and I know he needs to put them on. He probably needs help standing. His knee is in a stationary brace, his ankle must be sore, and he's not supposed to bear any weight. And he outweighs me by a hundred pounds.

"How's this going to work?" I ask him dumbly.

He grimaces. "I hate to ask you, but could you help? Or I can call the nurse…"

I shake my head immediately, rushing to grab the shorts. "Absolutely not. It's the least I can do."

I don't know why my hands shake as Brand pulls back the sheet. I don't know why I'm hesitant to look at his legs, which lead to his pelvis, which leads to his… Gah. No wonder my hands are shaky.

I grit my teeth and slide the leg hole over Brand's knee brace, as carefully as I can. I see him grit his teeth as I slide them up, over his bandaged thigh. I'm as careful as I can be, but I know it must still hurt.

My fingers graze the hot skin at his waist, and the smoothness of it is electrifying. It's silky and velvety at the same time as it is rock hard.

I suck in a breath as his fingers bump mine when he reaches for the waistband to finish pulling them up.

"Well, that was an Olympic maneuver," he says wryly. "Thanks."

I nod. "Where's your shirt?"

He gestures toward the chair, and I grab the black tee, tossing it to him. Taking a step, I untie his hospital gown, glancing at his muscle-bound back as I do.

A bald eagle flies across his shoulder blades, a ferocious expression on its face, its sharp talons exposed and ready to attack. Bold black letters are scrolled above it. *I stand on a wall to protect what is mine.*

Warmth rushes through me again, through all the hidden parts of me, at the idea of this fierce man protecting what is his.

I can't help but wonder what that must feel like. *To be his.* To stand within those strong arms, to kiss those full, firm lips. If I were his, I know he'd protect me until his dying breath. I could sleep every night without a fear, without a doubt. He'd keep the monsters at bay.

I shake the ridiculous thoughts away, and step back.

He's not mine.

Brand lets the hospital gown fall away and I inhale sharply.

Sweet Mary and all the saints.

God, I wish he were mine.

Washboard abs don't describe what Brand's got hidden under his shirt. His chest and stomach look like they're carved from bronze marble. How many hours in the gym does that even take??

He's got another tattoo on his chest, some sort of tribal symbol. It almost looks like a Japanese throwing star.

His bicep bulges as he moves, distracting me as he pulls his t-shirt over his head. Another tattoo is there on the flexing muscle. A skull in a beret over two crossed swords. *Death Before Dishonor.*

I gulp.

Is there anything sexier in the world than this man? Honorable, brave, strong. The trifecta of perfect male attributes.

I gasp when he pulls out his own IV, leaving it dangling on the bedrail.

"Holy crap," I breathe, eyeing the limp tube. "I could've gotten the nurse."

He rolls his eyes. "And we could've waited for an hour. It's fine. It's just pulling a needle out. Not exactly rocket science."

He blots at a tiny spot of blood, and I catch sight of yet another tattoo. I remember seeing it when he was pulling the debris off of me in the café, but I couldn't make out the words then, not through the smoke and the haze of my concussion. Without thinking, I pick up his arm and turn it over, exposing his forearm.

Black words scrawl from the wrist to the elbow.

Though I walk through the valley of death, I fear no evil.

My lady parts tingle.

This man is like catnip for my vagina.

I gulp. "I like your tattoos."

Brand glances up. "Yeah, I was lucky. Right after I discharged, they changed the rules. Said that officers can't have tattoos from their elbows to their wrists. I would've been screwed."

"I like them," I tell him softly, which is the biggest understatement in the history of the world. I fricking love them. They reveal so much about this man, more than I bet he wants people to know.

Honor. Bravery. Strength. Loyalty.

God. My nether-regions are tingling again.

"Thanks," Brand answers. He twists away to gather his things on the bed table and I realize that I had still been holding his arm as I pondered his many sexy traits.

Embarrassing.

A nurse comes to help transfer Brand to a wheelchair, and I watch how she does it, filing it away for future use. She also explains to him once again how to clean the wound on his thigh and lectures him one more time about not over-doing it.

"Now don't put any weight on that leg," she tells him sternly. "I don't want a repeat of last night."

I raise an eyebrow. "Last night?"

She shakes her head. "Mr. Killien is stubborn. He got up in the night by himself to go to the bathroom. Apparently, he didn't want to use his bedpan."

He snorts. "No one wants to use a bedpan."

She scowls at him. "No weight on that leg. Period. You can't break open your artery again, and you don't want to put weight on your knee and ankle." She looks at me. "You'll make sure, right?"

I nod quickly. To be honest, I'm a bit afraid of the stern old woman.

She wheels him down to the first floor and I trail behind with his sack of belongings. Glancing inside, I just find his pants that they cut off, his wallet and a phone.

I wonder if anyone has called him? If anyone has thought to look for him or check on him?

Because he seems so alone.

It tugs on the maternal place in my heart, the place that wants to keep him safe. He's obviously seen so much shit, so much terrible shit, all while 'standing on a wall' to protect me and everyone else in this country. Taking care of him now would be the least I could do.

And God, I want to be near him.

I want to breathe him in.

I want his goodness to fix me.

Please, God.

We slide the passenger seat of my car all the way back, and between the nurse, Brand and me, we get him situated. His long leg, encased in a knee brace, barely fits.

As I get in, I glance at him. "Just tell me where to go."

He nods. "Sure. We're headed to my friend's cottage out by the lake. I'll tell you where to turn."

"Okay." I head for the exit and Brand runs his finger along the leather-bound dashboard.

"Nice car," he tells me casually as I turn onto the highway.

I roll my eyes. "Thanks. I wanted a convertible, but my father thought that was too tacky."

"A Jaguar XJ isn't anything to sneeze at," he answers. "Although they're mechanical pieces of shit."

I snort back laughter. "Tell that to my father. He gave it to me as a graduation gift. I know, it's a grandma car."

"It is a little....geriatric," Brand grins. "But it's still nice."

It's the absolute story of my life. I want something, my father wants something else, and guess who wins that battle?

"Turn here," Brand tells me after a few minutes. Honeysuckle Drive.

"What a charming name," I muse aloud.

The road is just as charming as the name implies. Lined with shady trees, I idle down the quiet lane to the very end, to a little cottage perched on the lake. Cute and quaint, it's got vines growing up the side, a porch with two rocking chairs, and pots of flowers out front.

"This is a adorable," I observe before I get out and pull the wheelchair from the trunk.

I unfold it and push it over to the passenger side, but Brand scowls at it. "I'm not using that thing."

I scowl back. "Well, you certainly can't bear weight, and we don't have your crutches yet. So get into it, Killien."

Brand's head snaps up in surprise, then he bursts out laughing.

"A bit bossy, aren't you?" His eyes sparkle and it takes my breath away. "It's a good thing bossy looks good on you."

I smirk and hold the chair and Brand twists himself from the car and drops into it, all without managing to put weight on his leg. It's not without effort and I can see his face is a bit pale.

"We'll get you some pain pills in the house," I tell him. "The nurse said you could have one soon."

I wheel him to the door.

"The key is on top of the sill," he tells me. "Can you reach it?"

Barely.

But I manage, by stretching up on the very tip of my toes. When I turn back around, Brand is watching me, and heat floods my cheeks. His gaze had been fixed on my ass, on the way my shirt had pulled up as I stretched.

I *want* him to watch me, *to see me*, yet when he does, I get as flustered as the thirteen-year old I used to be. *Gah.*

I unlock the door and him inside.

The inside of the cottage is as cute as the outside, but it does have a pent-up musty smell and it's stifling hot.

"I'm going to open the windows," I tell Brand. "We need some air flowing. And I'll change the sheets on the bed for you. I'm guessing this cottage hasn't been opened up for the season."

"No, it hasn't," Brand agrees.

I push him over to the windows where he can look out over the lake while I wander about, opening windows, opening all the faucets to get fresh water flowing, and hunting for linens.

As I do, my phone rings in my pocket. I pull it out, staring at the screen, expecting to see my father or my mom, or even Nate.

But I don't.

My heart leaps into my throat, locking it up, when I see the name. I'm frozen for a minute, paralyzed. *You're an idiot. It's just a freaking phone call. He can't hurt you here.*

I will myself to move, and I'm finally able to shove the phone back into my pocket without answering it. But I feel it there, like a blazing piece of charcoal, taunting me.

I blink hard.

"You can answer that," Brand tells me, staring at me curiously. "I don't mind."

I shake my head. "It's no one important."

Only the devil himself.

Brand still stares at me. "Are you all right?"

No.

"Yes," I lie. "It's just hot in here. Opening the windows will help."

Trying to ignore the way my heart is pounding, I bring Brand a glass of water and one of his pain pills.

"I'll go into the pharmacy and get your prescription filled today," I tell him. "The hospital only sent ten pills. I'll pick up your crutches while I'm there."

Brand is already shaking his head. "No, you've already done enough. I'll suck it up and call my mother. I'm not your responsibility, Nora. I'm sure you've got better things to do."

But the look on his face. It stabs me in the heart because I know that look. I'm sure I have it myself whenever I speak of my father.

Brand could've died in surgery for all his mother knew, and she didn't even bother to come to the hospital. I'm outraged *for* him, enough so that I don't even think she deserves to be with him now. He's everything that's good in the world, and if she can't see that, then it's her loss.

"No," I insist. "It's not a trouble. Trust me, it's helping me out too. The more time I'm here, the less time I have to be at my parents' house."

I'm going to be here a lot, you just don't know it yet.

Brand starts to answer, but closes his mouth, nodding. His eyes hold a curious expression. I get that a lot. People always assume my life is all rainbows and butterflies. I'm rich, after all, right?

Well, money doesn't buy happiness.

Or good childhoods.

Or good fathers.

"I'm glad that's settled," I tell him firmly, taking back the glass and carrying it to the kitchen.

My phone buzzes again, this time with a text.

I don't want to look, I don't want to look, I don't want to look.

But I don't have the will power not to.

With my teeth gritted, I look.

Answer your phone.

I shudder, and slide my phone back into my pocket.

"Are you sure everything is ok?" Brand asks. He'd been watching me and I didn't even know it.

"Yeah."

No.

I'm not ok, because *the devil himself* can find me wherever I am.

I'm not safe.

I'm not safe.

But I'm safe with Brand...because he stands on a wall to protect what is his.

I rotate in a circle, taking the cottage in. Everything is on one floor here, so it'll be easier for Brand to get around. But he really shouldn't be alone. He can't even drive yet.

I suddenly know how to get what I want.

"I'm going to stay here with you," I announce, squaring my shoulders as I look at the sexy man in front of me.

His eyes widen and before he can argue, I continue.

"I insist. You can't cook for yourself, you can't walk, you can't drive. You don't want to talk to your mom and I get that. I wouldn't speak to my dad, if I could help it. Let me do this. I want to. I owe you. And if I'm here, then I don't have to see my dad. You'd actually be doing me a favor. Plus, I promised the nurse that I'd keep you off your leg."

I want to be here with you.

My eyes must tell him that. He stares into them, studying me, dissecting me. I feel like he's looking into me, figuring out all the broken parts.

But I'm studying him, too. And I see that while he's big and strong and brave, there's something in him that is hurting. I just don't know what it is yet. He's an enigma. And I can't wait to figure him out.

Finally, he nods slowly.

"If you really want to."

"I do," I tell him firmly, and my heart takes off like helicopter blades. "And when someone else comes, your girlfriend, or whatever, I'll just go back home. Easy-breezy."

Yes, it's a pathetic and blatant fishing attempt on my part.

Brand doesn't bite.

He eyes me and starts to say something, but then doesn't.

"Don't expect anyone for a while," he finally warns, an attempt to tell me that I might be here for a while, but still vague enough to not reveal anything about him.

That's fine. Because I'll be staying in a cottage with my teenage fantasy. Only he's not a fantasy anymore. And he's not a teenager. He's living, breathing, and sexy as hell.

And until he tells me that there's a girlfriend, I'm going to operate as if there isn't one.

For the next few weeks, Brand Killien is all mine.

That's plenty of time to figure all of his secrets out.

Chapter Four

Brand

From the armchair by the windows, I watch Nora unload her Jaguar. First she brings in a pair of crutches and leans them against my chair. Next she hauls in an overnight bag, then bag after bag of groceries before finally closing her trunk.

I hate sitting here like a helpless idiot while a woman carries in heavy groceries.

Jesus.

I fiddle with the crutches, adjusting them to the right height, before leaning them back against the chair.

Nora comes in and glances at me. "Okay. I didn't know what you liked, so I just got a variety of stuff. I also got you soda and beer. I took a guess on what kindsd you like."

I nod. "Anything will be fine. I'm not picky."

She stares at me sternly. "But you can't have the beer until you aren't taking the painkillers anymore."

I cock an eyebrow at her bossiness. "Yes, m'am."

Her face is flushed from the heat outside, her red hair coming loose from her chignon. I stare at all the groceries she'd just unpacked, then look back to her.

"Okay, a couple of questions. One, did you leave anything in the store?"

She rolls her eyes.

"Yes."

"And two, do you know how to cook?"

She rolls her eyes again.

"No. Not really. But how hard can it be?"

I snort. "Well, I can make eggs and frozen pizza. Did you get any pizzas?"

She shakes her head and now she's looking hesitant. "No. I didn't think of that."

The look on her face makes me smile. She's not used to not knowing how to do something, I can tell. And apparently, she's not used to taking care of herself.

"So, you can't cook, and I can't cook. And I can't walk," I make these observations with a smile.

She sniffs, turning up her nose before she walks away. "I also bought a cookbook."

She hears me laughing because her spine turns ramrod straight as she disappears into the kitchen. I'm still chuckling as I study my leg in the sun.

My knee hurts like a bitch. Obviously. Apparently, it turned backward and practically inside out.

My ankle throbs like a motherfucker too. It's swollen to the size of a football.

My pain medicine is in the kitchen, where Nora is putting away all of those groceries alone, and right now, it looks like a hundred miles from here to there.

Suck it up, Buttercup.

With a groan, I grab the crutches next to me, and heft myself up, managing to not put weight on my leg.

Fucking-A.

It takes me five full minutes to make the trip. When I round the corner, Nora is stretching up on her toes to put food in the cabinets. Her shirt has pulled up, showing her flat stomach.

"Hey," she looks up, yanking her shirt down. "You shouldn't be up."

"I've got an injured leg. I'm not an invalid," I tell her grumpily, because invalid or not, my leg is throbbing like hell. I eye my pain pills, which are mocking me from

47

above the sink, twenty painful steps away. I start my slow hobble toward them.

"Did you need something? I could've gotten it for you," she tells me quickly, setting down a jar of spaghetti sauce, and heading for me.

I'm already shaking my head.

"You're not my servant," I tell her. "I'm not sure why you wanted to be here so bad, but you're not going to wait on me hand and foot." My words are sharper than I meant for them to be, but shit. My fucking leg hurts.

Nora's mouth snaps closed and she looks like I slapped her. I feel guilty, because I know she only wants to help, but I don't say anything. I'm tired, I'm in pain, I'm pissed at the world. It's probably best that I just keep my mouth shut.

Without another word, I reach for the pills. Unfortunately, I'm not used to my crutches yet, and the left one rolls out from under me.

I lose my balance, and in my effort to not land on my leg, I slam into Nora, effectively pinning her to the counter.

She looks up at me, her eyes wide.

She's so small compared to me, as I tower above her. Awkwardly, I shift my weight so I'm not smashing her, but I don't move completely away.

Because my pelvis likes being pushed into her pelvis.

Her heat emanates into me, and she stares up into my eyes.

"You don't want me here?" she asks breathily, her fingers curled around the counter edge. Her knuckles are white.

"I didn't say that," I answer quietly, still not moving. Because right now, with her soft curves pressed into me, I do want her here.

And unfortunately, my dick chooses this moment to agree with me.

It hardens against her and her eyes widen.

"I see," she murmurs.

I rotate away, straightening up and leaning on my crutches once again.

"Sorry about that," I tell her. "I hope I didn't crush you."

With my hard-on.

Her mouth twitches. "No worries. Let's get you back out to your chair and I'll bring you your pills."

I don't argue, I simply turn and begin the slow hobble to my chair.

Nora follows at my elbow, and as I'm twisting to drop into the chair, she gasps.

"Holy shit, Brand," she breathes. "Your leg."

I glance down and find a large spot of blood spreading on my inner thigh.

Fuck. I must've jostled the sutures in the kitchen.

Without another word, Nora bends over me, yanking the elastic band of my shorts down. I lift my hips to let the shorts slide down, and Nora's cool fingertips find my inner thigh.

I grit my teeth.

Not because of pain, because there isn't any. But because Nora's fingers are literally a couple of inches away from my dick.

Cold fish. Cold fish. Cold fish.

Cold.

Fucking.

Fish.

"You broke open your wound," she says needlessly, her voice panicked. She pulls at the blood-soaked bandage, examining the injury. She covers it with the gauze again, pressing her fingers firmly to it for a long moment before looking at it again.

"Okay. I think it's fine. It was just a little tear, and it stopped bleeding." She looks up at me, her face calmer now. "But you've got to be more careful, especially these first few days. If you need something, call me. Don't try to get it yourself."

I nod curtly, but I'd probably agree with anything right about now. Her fingers are pressed to my groin again and she's kneeling in front of me. My thoughts aren't on my fucking injury.

In fact, my thoughts are *far* from my fucking injury, but thankfully, I'm saved by someone clearing their throat in the doorway.

Nora and I both turn at the same time.

My mother stands there, her face disapproving, her shoulders stiff.

"Am I interrupting?" she asks icily.

I stare at her hard, because I haven't seen her in nine years, because no one invited her here, and because she didn't even bother to knock.

Bethany Killien is smaller, frailer and grayer than she was nine years ago.

Her thin arms stay at her sides. She doesn't approach me, she doesn't reach for me, she simply stands there, limp and quiet. Her face is tired, her hair pulled into a bun at her neck. She looks like someone who has lived a thousand lives.

"No, you're not interrupting," I tell her coolly, while Nora scrambles to get up. I don't acknowledge the fact that Nora was on her knees in front of me, or that I'm in my underwear. I know what it might look like.

But it's none of my mother's business.

"Well, I see that you're deep in grief," she says curtly, "so I won't stay long. I just brought your truck down for you. The mayor brought it to my house after the

50

explosion. There's some fire damage to one side of it, but it still runs."

My mother stares pointedly at Nora, and Nora looks at me.

"Should I give you a few minutes?" she asks quietly, staring only at me. She acts like my mother doesn't even exist. I could hug her for that.

I nod. "Yeah, that's fine."

She regally walks past my mother without another word or glance.

Again, I could fucking hug her for that.

I stare at my mother, who hasn't moved even an inch toward me. I don't bother asking how she knew I was here. I just cut to the chase.

"Well, are you going to come in and tell me why you need me? I assume you need something or you wouldn't have bothered calling me."

I hate that I sound so bitter and hateful. I hate that she's done this to me. I hate that I've *let* her do this to me.

I try and swallow the hate.

It won't hurt anyone but me.

My mother walks into the room and sits at the chair across from me, holding her small body stiff. There's no maternal concern here. She doesn't bother to ask how I am.

It's only now that I notice she's carrying something. She places a wooden box on her lap and stares at me.

"It's your father's will," she says simply. "You're the sole heir."

Shock slams into me like a Mack truck, and I stare at her in confusion. Her face is a steel mask, unyielding, expressionless.

"There's no way, " I manage to say. "Why would he do that?"

She shrugs.

"I'm as surprised as you are. After everything you did, I don't understand it either."

Everything you did.

The words linger in the air between us and I swallow hard, trying to contain my hate. I don't bother to try and defend myself. It doesn't make any sense anymore. My father is gone, so what difference does it make? There's no point.

But that doesn't mean that I deserve her resentment.

"I don't want anything of his," I tell her icily. "Not his shop, not his truck, not anything."

She stares at me, her brown eyes hard. "So you're telling me that everything he left you... the shop, his truck, his bike, even the house... you don't want any of it?"

I level my gaze at her. "That's exactly what I'm saying."

I pause, thinking of his bike. A glistening, aggressive 1964 Triumph. It was my grandfather's before it was my father's, and my grandfather meant for it to come to me.

"I want the bike," I amend. "I don't want anything else. You can have it. Or burn it. I don't care."

My mother stares at me in satisfaction. Obviously, that's what she came to hear.

She holds out the box.

I stare at it. It's a cube made from ebony wood, with an ivory inlay in the wood. My name is carved into the ivory.

"Your father made this for you out in his woodshop," my mother says. "He left it with the estate attorney, along with the will."

I don't move to take it from her. "I don't want it," I tell her firmly.

She looks away in disgust. "Your father must've worked hours on that. I don't know why. But he meant for you to have it, and you're going to have it." She sets it on the floor at her feet before looking back up at me. "I don't know why he chose to forgive you, Branden. But I never will."

I taste bile and red bleeds into my vision as the hatred swells through my chest and pumps through my veins.

"You don't know what you think you know," I manage to say thickly, every word like ice. "Now get out."

She steps over the box and walks stiffly toward the door. Once there, she turns.

"I'll send the papers over for you to sign once they're ready."

I turn away and look out the windows.

I hear the door close.

I taste the bitterness in my mouth. I feel my heart beat, pushing the hatefulness through my limbs before it returns to my heart, poisoning it.

But I don't feel anything else. I'm numb.

"Are you okay?" Nora asks softly from the door. "I couldn't hear what was going on, but you don't look okay."

She walks over to me, and picks up the box.

"This is beautiful," she observes gently. "What's in it?"

I shrug as if I don't care. "I don't know."

She starts to take the lid off, but I stop her.

"Don't, please."

My words are soft but firm. Nora stops in surprise, her fingers poised on the lid.

"Okay." She sets it on a table by the sofa, across the room from me. It seems to mock me and I look away.

I don't want to know yet what my father had to say. I don't know if I ever will.

"Thanks," I tell her. She looks down at me and her eyes are filled with understanding. I don't know how, but she seems to get it.

Although she can't possibly. No one can.

"No problem," she says gently. "Now, on to more urgent matters. What should I try to make for dinner?"

I chuckle at the look of utter fear on her face. "Have you never had to cook for yourself?"

She shakes her head. "At my parent's house, we have a housekeeper. When I was away at college, I ate in the dorms, and then when I moved to an apartment in grad school, I had takeout."

"I'm doomed, then, is what you're telling me?" I ask, trying to lighten the mood. She laughs.

"I'm going to try something easy. Meat loaf. After it's in the oven, I'm going to take a quick dip in the lake to cool off. Do you need anything beforehand?"

I shake my head. "Nah, I'm good. Unless you could get me a book?"

She grabs one from the shelves on the far wall, and hands it to me before she disappears into the kitchen. I concentrate on reading, rather than focusing on the pain throbbing in my leg, or the fucking wooden box mocking me from across the room.

Nora emerges thirty minutes later, looking a bit frazzled, but otherwise, no worse for the wear.

"Okay," she announces triumphantly. "We have a loaf made from meat baking. I don't know if it'll be edible, but it's baking. I'm headed out to the lake. Hopefully the water will wash out the hamburger under my fingernails. Otherwise, it might be there permanently."

I smile. "Enjoy yourself."

She glances at me before she heads to her bedroom to change. "After your thigh heals, maybe we could get you out there? It might be a good way for you to exercise since you don't have to bear weight."

Alarm floods me, quick and white-hot and I immediately shake my head.

"I don't swim."

Nora stares at me in surprise. "You can't, or don't?"

"I don't."

She's clearly puzzled, but she doesn't pry. "Ok. It was just an idea."

"I know," I tell her, my pulse still bounding wildly in my throat. "Thank you."

She nods and leaves and I stare out the window again, calming down.

Stop being a pussy.

But God, it's hard. The *one thing* I can't get past. I was able to get past the bullets and explosions of Afghanistan, for God's sake.

But not this.

At the mere thought of it, my heart pounds in my chest, threatening to break free from my ribcage.

With a deep breath, I watch the water, rippling peacefully against the shore, in a fluid age-old motion, a harmless, serene motion.

It's harmless, you fucking pussy.

But I know that it isn't always.

As I stare at the familiar landscape, I'm filled with trepidation.

I don't like being home. Being here brings back memories, and uncomfortable feelings.... things I would just as soon keep buried.

Home. Most people take comfort in being back home. Home is a place they always feel safe, secure and loved.

Too bad I'm not most people.

I felt safer in the battlefields of Afghanistan than I did here.

Quit being such a fucking girl.

With a sigh, I turn my attention back to the book, scrolling through each page, until a movement outside distracts me an hour or so later.

Nora is wading out of the lake and onto the beach. She looks like a sea nymph or a siren as she swings her long wet hair out of her face, and the sun envelops her body, glistening on every wet plane.

Her thighs are long, her tits are full and perky and she's practically naked now, fully wet as the water streams over her body.

My dick tightens in reaction and I suck in my breath.

Through the window, Nora's eyes meet mine and I'm not sure what I see hidden in hers. Determination, I think.

But what exactly is she determined to do?

As I watch her bend to get her towel, I'm not sure I want to find out, although my penis seems to disagree. *He's* interested in every little thing Nora Greene does.

He doesn't know what he's getting us into.

To be honest, I don't know either.

Chapter Five

Nora

As I change out of my bathing suit and into a sundress, I ponder the look on Brand's face.

Hesitant.

Reluctant.

But why?   I saw him watch me. I know that at least part of him wants me.

Butterflies flutter in my belly at that thought. *Brand Killien wants me.*

But he doesn't *want* to want me.

That's just as obvious and it quiets the butterflies back down. I stare glumly in the mirror as I comb my wet hair. There must be a reason, and it more than likely has to do with a woman. Brand is loyal as the day is long, I can tell. So there must be a girlfriend.

With a sigh, I put down my comb and head out to the kitchen.

Good Lord, the heat. The hot oven has turned the kitchen into a freaking inferno. Lesson one. *Don't use the oven on a hot day.*

It's even hotter as I open the oven and pull out the meat. Which, incidentally, is charred.

What the hell?

I poke at it and find that the top and bottom are covered in a blackened crust. Only the middle is edible and I have no idea why. I did everything the recipe said to do.   Crap.   Excerpt set the oven timer. I baked it thirty minutes longer than I was supposed to.

I'm blowing the hair out of my face when Brand calls in to me.

"How's it coming?"

I don't want to admit defeat. But I'm sure the man is hungry.

I slink out with my tail between my legs.

"I've got many talents," I announce. "Unfortunately, it seems that cooking isn't one of them. Yet."

Brand bursts out laughing, setting his book on his lap. I flush as I remember his lap shoved against me earlier. And how happy his *lap* had been to see mine.

"Take-out?" he suggests.

I nod. "Takeout. Any ideas?"

"Actually, yes," he tells me. "I was actually here last year for dinner. Some friends of mine owned the little Italian place and I came here one evening. They sold it, but I believe it still serves the same menu. Italian sounds good to me."

"It does to me too," I tell him as I grab my purse. "Especially since I won't have to cook it."

Brand tosses me his wallet. "It's on me."

I don't argue, because I know there would be no point. I can already tell that he's stubborn.

I head for The Hill. I've actually eaten there many times throughout the summers.

Like always, it's packed tonight with hungry tourists. I patiently wait my turn to order at the take-out counter, and when it's finally my turn, an older Italian woman smiles at me.

"Hello there, welcome to the Hill. What can I get for you?"

I give her our order, and she rings it up. "That will be eighteen dollars and twenty-four cents."

I open Brand's wallet and pull out the money, but the woman's eyes are frozen on his driver's license picture.

"Do you know Brand?" she asks me, her face lighting up. Surprised, I nod.

"Yes. You do too?"

She nods happily. "That's a good man, sweetie. After my husband Tony died, Brand came to the funeral, but then he came back with his friend Gabe to haul my daughter's stuff to college. That's a good family, bella."

I'm confused. "But he and Gabe aren't related, right?"

The woman laughs. "They might as well be. Well, he and Gabe. He and Jacey on the other hand… aye yi yi."

That snags my attention, but she's holding out her hand now. "I'm Maria, bella. And you?"

I shake her hand. "Nora." I purposely leave off the Greene. "It's a pleasure. What were you saying about Brand and Jacey?"

Maria eyes me knowingly. "He and that girl. Jacey means well, but she never could get her head on straight. Always made bad choices. One of her ex-boyfriends killed my Tony, you know. Ran him right off the road. Brand tried to get her straightened out, and we all know why. He was head over heels for that girl. But she married someone else. Some famous actor. I never could understand why, probably another bad choice. Because Brand's the cream of the crop, honey. She's crazy for not wanting him. Let me tell you, if Brand's interested in you, you'd better keep him."

Maria stares at me pointedly and I realize that I'm holding Brand's wallet, paying for a dinner for two with it. Of course she thinks there might be something to that. But I can't focus on that, mainly because I know Brand doesn't want me. Or he doesn't *want* to want me, anyway.

"Which actor did Jacey marry, Maria?" I ask curiously.

She wrinkles her nose in disdain. "Dominic Kinkaide."

I recognize the name immediately, and picture him in my head. Hollywood's most famous bad-boy.

I've seen his face a thousand times in the movies. Tall, dark and dangerous. But at the same time, I do remember seeing photos of he and his new bride plastered on the tabloids.

Jacey Vincent-Kinkaide. Blonde, brown-eyed. Gorgeous.

Brand was in love with someone who is the polar opposite of me.

And he might very well still be, for all I know. Maybe *that's* why he doesn't want to want me. He doesn't have a girlfriend, but he's still in love with someone else.

I swallow hard.

"It's been nice meeting you, Maria," I tell her as she hands me the dinner bags. "I'm sure I'll be in a lot this summer."

She smiles. "Tell Brand hello for me, dear. I hope to see him, too."

I shake my head as I head out to the car. Maria is very genuine. She truly wants to see Brand. Apparently, Brand has the same effect on everyone. They want to be near him, to soak him up. At least it isn't just me.

Brand is waiting at the table when I get back to the cottage, and the table is set for two. I shake my head as I carry in the bags.

"You're so stubborn. You're supposed to rest. It isn't that hard for most people, Brand."

He shrugs. "I guess I'm not most people."

Hell no, you're not.

I dish our food onto real plates, and push one across the table to him.

"So, Maria was really nice."

Brand looks up and grins. "You met Maria? She's a sweet lady. Don't let her fool you, though. Her husband died last year. She's hard as nails."

I take a bite of lasagna, trying to act casual.

"Yeah, she mentioned that Tony died. She mentioned a lot....about you, and Gabe and Jacey."

Brand looks up at me, but he doesn't show any reaction. "She did, huh?"

I nod. "Yeah. She said that Jacey's ex ran Tony off the road."

Brand sighs and takes a bite of his food. "Yeah. It was a hard time. Jacey didn't always make good decisions. But she's doing better now."

"Yeah, Maria mentioned that, too. And that's she's married to Dominic Kinkaide."

Again, Brand shows no reaction.

"Yep. In fact, I think they're in Europe right now. You probably won't see her this summer."

This causes my head to snap up. "Why would I see her?"

Brand looks at me in surprise. "This is her cabin. Well, she shares it with Gabe. Like I mentioned, they inherited it from their grandparents."

He'd mentioned his friends had inherited it. He hadn't said that one of the friend's was Jacey Vincent-Kinkaide.

"Oh." I feel a bit deflated. I don't know why. He might be in love with Jacey, but she's married. To one of the world's most famous actors. And she's thousands of miles away right now. She's not a threat to me. *Brand can't have her.*

We eat in comfortable silence and after I clear away our leftovers, I turn to Brand.

"There's no cable here."

He smiles. "I know. It used to drive us crazy in the summers."

"I can imagine. But I saw a checkers board in one of the bookcases. Do you want to sit outside and play?"

Brand stares at me in surprise. "Sure. I just never figured you for a board games girl."

I roll my eyes. "You don't know me yet."

Yet.

I set the game up and Brand hobbles out on his crutches. Even injured, his biceps bulge and flex with each movement. I could watch his arms all day. But I can't. I've got a game to play…in more ways than one.

Instead, I look up. "Black or red?"

Brand sits down. "Black."

"Then you go first," I suggest. "But I've got a caveat…something that will make the game more interesting."

Brand raises a blond eyebrow. "Oh, yeah? And what's that? Strip checkers?"

I smirk. "You wish. But no. If one of us gets jumped, the other one gets to ask a question. And we have to answer."

Brand cocks his head. "Clever. What if we don't really want to know the answers? Sometimes mystery is better than reality."

I shake my head. "I disagree. There are things I'm dying to know about you."

Brand rolls his eyes. "I'm not that interesting."

"Let me decide that," I suggest. "Your move….if you're not afraid."

He snorts, and I push the board toward him. He moves a black checker forward.

Then I move a red one.

We go back and forth a few times, until he manages to jump one of mine.

"Bingo," he says with a grin.

"Wrong game," I tell him. "What's your question?"

He thinks on that, his large hand drumming on his thigh. "Hmm. Let's see. Okay, why are you spending the summer here in Angel Bay?"

I answer immediately. "My father wanted me to take the summer off and recharge my batteries. I just finished law school."

"So your brain is tired?" Brand grins and I swear, it could light up the entire lake. I nod.

"I guess you could say that."

"Your move," he tells me.

I move. Then he moves. We parry back and forth, until I finally manage to jump him.

"Do you love Jacey?"

I'm not one to beat around the bush. Brand's head snaps back and he stares at me in disbelief.

"Wow. You don't mess around, do you?"

"No. Maria talked so much about her that I'm curious. What's your answer?" I stare into his eyes and he stares back. Finally he nods and for a minute, my heart stops beating. But then he clarifies.

"Yes. But not in the romantic way. I thought I did for a while, but maybe I never did. She and Gabe have been like my family. I was close to her, and maybe I got confused. Emotions aren't my forte."

"So you don't love her romantically?"

Brand shakes his head. "That's two questions, sweetheart."

I suck in my breath at the endearment, and Brand smirks. "What? No one's ever called you that?"

He's kidding, but I shake my head. "No."

"You're joking."

Brand is dumbfounded now and I have to laugh. "No, I'm not kidding. Believe it or not, I haven't had that many relationships. My father never approves of anyone."

Brand stares at me drolly. "But you were away at college. What your father didn't know wouldn't have hurt him."

I almost shudder. "My father knows everything. Trust me. It's your turn."

Brand drops it, and goes, much to my relief. I don't want to get into how my father kept tabs on me at school. Before long, Brand jumps me again. He levels a blue, blue gaze at me.

"Are you happy?" he asks thoughtfully, rocking back in his seat with his good leg. I suck in a breath.

"Blunt, aren't you?"

He chuckles. "No more than you."

Touché.

"No, not really," I answer honestly. "I hope to be someday."

Brand stares at me hard. "Why aren't you happy now?"

"That's two questions," I throw his words back at him. "It's my turn to go."

Brand rolls his eyes, but I ignore him as I move.

I jump him two moves later.

"What happened in Afghanistan?"

He doesn't even flinch. "My HUMVEE was bombed. My leg was shattered."

"You earned a purple heart," I tell him. "So I know there's more to the story."

He shrugs. "I don't think it serves any purpose to talk about it. Some memories are best left alone. I've dealt with it and moved on, but that doesn't mean I enjoy thinking about it."

There's a look on his face, a *don't fuck with me* look, that I decide to heed. "Your turn," I tell him softly instead. He nods.

He moves a checker, only to open himself up to a double-jump. I crow and jump him. Twice. He glares at me mockingly.

"I don't like this game."

I giggle. "I get two questions."

He doesn't argue, he just crosses his arms and waits.

"There's something bothering you, I see it on your face. I have a feeling that it's not your dad's death, and you say you've dealt with Afghanistan, so what is it?"

Brand looks away. "I really don't like this game."

I smile, but I don't back off. "What's your answer?"

He stares out the window for a minute, at the lake, before he sighs. "Sometimes bad things happen in life. Sometimes they happen when you're really young. Those are the memories that won't fade with time."

I'm stunned. It's a vague answer, but it's still oh-so revealing. Something happened to him when he was a kid, something bad.

"Do you want to talk about it?" I ask gently.

Brand looks at me. "That was your second question, you know."

I nod. "That's fine. What's your answer?"

He shakes his head immediately. "No. I don't want to talk about it. I'm a grown fucking man, not a pussy. I don't need to talk about it."

"Yet it still bothers you,' I state simply.

"There's no fix for it," he tells me firmly. "My father's dead. I guess that's all the closure I need."

I'm doubtful as I stare at Brand's gorgeous face. His gorgeous, tortured face. He doesn't have closure. I can see that right now. I don't know what to think about his family situation. He doesn't seem to be grieving, but he's

65

still troubled about something. Deeply troubled. But I can also see that he's done talking about it.

"Your turn," I say instead. He goes. I go.

After he goes again, I manage to jump him.

"What do you do for a living?"

He grins, pretending to be relieved, only maybe it's not an act. I can tell he doesn't like to talk about himself. At all.

"Gabe and I started a company together a couple of years ago. We developed military grade body armor. We started the company to keep soldiers safer, but it's also being used by police departments and private security details."

"That sounds amazing," I tell him softly. And it sounds like exactly something he would do...*keeping people safe.* He shrugs.

"It's a living."

He pushes away from the little table. "I'm about done in for the day," he tells me. "Thank you for going to get dinner, Nora. And I'm sorry you're not happy. Hopefully you can figure that out soon."

He hobbles away and I have to agree with the sentiment.

Hopefully I can figure that out soon.

Chapter Six

Nora

I put away the checkers, and boot up my laptop, checking a few emails. My mother has written four.

You're only five minutes away. Can't you come home for tea soon?

Your father isn't happy about your current situation.

Yeah, what's new?

But it's her last email that sends ice water through my veins, chilling every part of me.

William called yesterday, wanted to know where you were. He said you weren't returning his phone calls and that he had some business related questions for you. I told him where you are, but told him that you were taking the summer off. I hope that was okay.

I take a ragged breath.

Then another.

I told him where you are.

He knows where I am.

With shaking fingers, I answer her email.

I'm sorry. Like I told you the other day, I feel responsible for Brand. He got injured because of me. I'll definitely come home soon for tea. It's okay that you told William where I am. I'm sure he just has a simple question or something.

It's not okay. Not at all.

But she doesn't know what he did.

I hit 'send' and close my laptop.

As I walk through the house, I find Brand sitting in front of the windows again. Instead of staring out at the lake, his gaze is firmly fixed on the box his mother had brought. It stands out starkly against the white wood that it's sitting on.

He's staring at it so intently that he doesn't even realize I'm watching him.

The look on his face is painful. Intent, hurt, vulnerable.

I can only imagine what might've happened to him in the past. But from the way he's staring at that freaking box, it must have something to do with his father.

With a sigh, I continue on to the kitchen to make some hot tea.

I guess we both have secrets.

I keep mine closed away in the furthest, darkest place in my heart. I'm sure Brand does the same. I'm also sure that I'll never know about them until he's good and ready to share.

Sipping at my tea, I slouch in a kitchen chair. Looking around, I try and imagine the days when this cozy little cabin was bustling with life. Apparently, Jacey and Gabe spent every summer here with their grandparents, and Brand was here a lot.

Because I'd done a little bit of digging, I know that Brand's parents' house is just down the road. When we drove here, he didn't even point it out.

There's bad blood there, obviously. I just can't imagine what a guy like him could possibly have done to make his own parents turn on him.

The sound of the shower running jars me from my thoughts and I look up in alarm. Brand isn't supposed to get the dressings on his thigh wet. *God, he's stubborn.*

I leap out of the chair and sprint down the hall, throwing open the bathroom door.

Brand is completely naked, balanced against the bathroom sink as he prepares to maneuver himself into the shower.

He's surprised to see me, and I'm frozen as I stare at him.

He's absolutely beautiful naked.

It's like he's been sculpted from marble by a skilled master. Michelangelo, perhaps. I suck in a breath, unable to take my eyes away from him.

Rippled abs.

Chiseled pecs.

Thighs like steel.

And then, then…

My eyes travel south.

Dear Lord.

Brand clears his throat. "My eyes are up here, Miss Greene."

I flush a thousand shades of red as I yank my gaze up to meet his. His eyes are filled with amusement…at my expense.

He lifts an eyebrow. "Can I help you?"

"You're not supposed to shower," I stammer. "You're supposed to sponge off this week. Remember?"

Brand rolls his eyes with a sigh.

"I don't need to remember. Apparently you remember for me."

I toss him a towel and regrettably, he wraps it around his hips, hiding his glorious body before he grabs his crutches.

"I don't have the first clue how to take a sponge bath," he grumbles as he limps past me.

"Me either," I tell him. "But we can figure it out."

We.

The butterflies start flying again, hard and fast, in my stomach. Brand turns to look at me.

"We?"

I nod. "Yeah. What kind of nurse would I be if I didn't help? Go lie down on your bed. I'll be there in a minute with the stuff."

Brand rolls his eyes and mutters beneath his breath, but he hobbles away. I rush to the kitchen and get a huge bowl of warm water before I stop at the hall closet for washcloths, towels and soap. My hands shake the entire time.

What the hell am I doing?

Why is he letting me do it?

He must want me to.

That knowledge, that theory, fuels me on and forces me into his bedroom. My window of opportunity to be with this man is closing by the day.

I can't waste it.

Grow a pair, Nora.

I set the bowl down on his nightstand and glance down. He's reclining on his back, his towel covering his midriff and groin. His hands are behind his head and he's every inch casual and cool as he waits for me.

I wonder if he's as anxious on the inside as I am?

Of course not. Because he doesn't know what I have planned.

He glances at me.

"So, where do we start?"

His voice is husky and sexy and....gah. I want to run out of the room and hide in my own, because I don't know what I'm doing here.

I only know what I want.

I want him.

"We start by washing off your arms," I tell him, calmly and professionally, as I move to his side. He grins up at me.

"Sure." He holds his arm up. "Go ahead, nurse."

I take a breath, grab the cloth, and run it along the hardened contours of his arm. Where most people are soft, he's as solid as a rock.

"Other one," I say softly, re-wetting the cloth. I circle the bed and wash the other one, the one with the tattoo on his forearm.

Though I walk through the valley of death, I fear no evil.

"Were you scared overseas?" I ask candidly as I run the cloth over the words. Brand opens his eyes.

"Of course."

Of course. It was a stupid question. It just doesn't seem like he'd be scared of anything.

"Being brave doesn't mean not being afraid, Nora," Brand tells me, lifting his ocean blue eyes to meet mine. "It means being afraid and doing it anyway."

"Doing *it*?" I ask.

Brand shrugs. "*It* can be anything. Whatever it is that you're doing, whatever it is that you're afraid of."

I'm doing *this*. Right now.

Because I want him. I want him this summer and he's not getting it. He's not making any moves even though I'm here and I'm available, and I want him. There's only one way to make him see... I have to be as blunt as a man.

I can do this.

Because I'm brave.

I'm brave.

I'm brave.

I'm fucking brave.

I re-wet my cloth and without a word of warning, I pull the corner of his towel back, then pull it entirely off.

Brand's eyes fly open, then fix on my face. He doesn't say a word, but I can see him holding his breath. His flat abdomen isn't moving.

I dip the cloth down his side, over the rippled muscle. I can feel him through the cloth, his warmth soaking into my fingers.

I pass his hip, his delicious, sexy hip. In my head, I envision it flexing as he straddles me. I flush, and gulp.

I'm brave.

I'm fucking brave.

I take a breath, and my fingers keep moving. Another breath and the cloth glides downward.

Then Brand's hand covers my own, stopping me.

"I think I can get that part."

I look down at him, and he's staring at me in apprehension....because he doesn't know what I'm doing... or what I want. I don't know either. All I know is....I'm doing it now. Before it's too late and he's out of my life and I never have another chance.

"Brand, I have a proposition to make."

My words cut the slice through the tension.

He levels a gaze at me, his eyes so fucking blue. "I'm listening."

His hand is still covering mine. It's warm and strong and I can hear the pulse rushing through my ears in a roar.

"I've wanted you since I was twelve years old. You're here for the summer and so am I. I don't know if I'll ever see you again and I don't want to look up from my desk at Greene Corp when I'm seventy and have regrets because I didn't do this."

I pause and Brand doesn't say anything.

He simply waits.

The silence between us is charged and I rush my next words...I let them tumble from my mouth before I lose the nerve.

"I want you. Without any strings at all. At the end of the summer, we'll probably never see each other again...but I want this summer. With you."

I have to know what's its like.

I stand on a wall and protect what is mine.

I need to know, even if it's just an illusion, what it's like to be his.

To be safe.

To be good.

Please.

Brand stares at me, stunned.

I'm stunned too.

I did it.

I did it.

I'm fucking brave.

I watch his lips slowly part as he breathes out in a rush.

I watch his tongue dart out and lick his lower lip.

I feel the heat from his hand as he slightly moves it.

Then I watch the word form on his mouth...right before he says it.

"No."

Chapter Seven

Brand

Nora stares at me, stunned. Her blue eyes are wide and clear, and I see hurt in them. Hurt that I put there without meaning to.

"No?" she repeats shakily, confused. She wasn't expecting that answer. I wasn't expecting to say it, to be honest. If I were smart, I'd take her up on her offer and have a summer-long sex session.

But as I look at her now, she seems more vulnerable and sad than confident and commanding as she'd want the world to think. A part of me knows that strings-free sex is the last thing she needs.

"No," I answer again. "Jesus, Nora. You're worth more than that."

She flushes bright red and yanks her hand away as if my skin were on fire. "You don't know me," she snaps as she gathers the sponge bath supplies. "You don't know what I'm worth, or what I want, Brand. Get over yourself."

She grabs my towel off the floor and tosses it back to me. I grasp her elbow, holding her still as I sit up.

"Nora, I didn't mean to insult you. You're a beautiful, sexy woman. I don't know why you feel like meaningless sex with me this summer would be smart, but I get the feeling that it's the last thing you need. You're worth more than a hollow fuck."

She flinches away at my words, but that's something about me. I'm always honest.

"It wouldn't be meaningless," she murmurs, looking into my face. "I've wanted you for years. Being with you now would be like fulfilling my oldest fantasy before I have to immerse myself in my father's business. What's wrong with that? Don't I deserve to do something that I want to do before I have to hand my life to my father?"

I'm the one recoiling now as I stare at her in shock. I'm her fantasy? What kind of nonsense is this? If the situation weren't so tense, I'd laugh.

"I'm not exactly fantasy material," I tell her instead, fighting to keep from smiling. "I'm just the son of a mechanic who joined the Army and got out of this one-horse town. Not really the stuff of fairy tales, Nora. And besides, you aren't handing your life to your father. You're going to work for him. Your life will still be your own."

She shakes her head. "You don't know anything about me, Brand. Or my life."

With that, she walks out, leaving me alone in the room with only a towel covering my dick.

I feel like I've been steam-rolled.

What the actual fuck was that?

I roll off the bed, put my clothes back on, and hobble out to follow Nora, but when I reach the hall, I hear water running. She's in the shower....where she's wet and naked.

I need a beer.

Fuck not being able to drink a beer and take a pain pill at the same time.

It takes five minutes to get to the kitchen, but when I do, I take the pill with a swig of beer, raising the bottle in Nora's direction.

Cheers.

I gulp down the rest of the icy liquid, letting it trickle down my throat and chill it's way into my belly.

As I'm internally patting myself on the back because I've gotten one over on Nurse Nora, her phone buzzes on the kitchen counter. I lean over and look out of idle curiosity.

I suck my breath in at what I see.

Four new texts from someone named William.

Answer your fucking phone.

Goddamnit, Nora.

I know where you are.

You don't know what I'm capable of. I want your word. If you're smart, you'll give it to me, and you'll keep it.

I stare at the harsh words and try to reconcile them with the Nora that I know so far. She's clearly someone who is driven and ambitious, but that's who she is on the outside. I also can see that on the inside, she's vulnerable and soft. I have no clue what she might've done to set this guy off.

Is he a business associate? Someone she's dealing with at Greene Corp? A business deal?

But he's threatening her. *I know where you are.*

What kind of colleague would threaten over a business deal?

I set her phone back down, just in time for Nora to walk into the kitchen, in only her towel.

I turn, and then freeze when I see her.

Creamy white shoulders, soft skin, long legs.

I swallow hard and meet her gaze.

"Who's William?" I ask simply. Her eyes grow guarded.

She leans around me, purposely pressing her towel-clad front against me. Her soft curves fold into me, sexy and warm. I feel her nipples poke me through the towel and my groin reacts.

The corners of her mouth turn up. "Does it matter?"

She looks up at me, grinning impishly now, her face inches from my crotch.

"Is there anything you need while I'm down here?"

My dick twitches.

"No," I tell her firmly, pulling her up by her upper arms. "Who's William?"

She sighs. "Someone from work. It's fine."

But it's not fine. I can see it on her face, I can tell by the way she drains of color at the mere mention of his name. But her shoulders are back and her chin is out. She's determined not to talk about him.

That's fine.

We all have our secrets.

She smiles triumphantly when I drop the subject and she grabs her phone, spins around, and drops her towel. It falls at my feet.

She walks confidently out the door, as naked as the day she was born.

Her legs flex as she walks, and her ass is round and firm and my dick reacts once again.

Fuck.

I groan and look away.

I can hear Nora chuckling from the other room and I roll my eyes.

I also hear her turn off the shower.

Apparently, she's changed her mind about taking one.

She pops her head back into the kitchen.

"Want to go skinny-dipping?"

Yes.

"No," I tell her firmly. "I don't swim."

"So you said," she nods, then struts through the kitchen naked, opens the back door, and makes her way across the lawn in the broad daylight to the private beach behind the house.

I shake my head, unable to prevent the smile from spreading across my face.

The girl is something, that's for sure.

I limp to the window and watch her.

She's unconcerned that someone will see her. She simply doesn't care as she puts on her show for me.

And it's for me. I know that.

Nora isn't the kind of girl to strut outside nude in the daylight for any other reason than a means to her end. For whatever reason, she's made it her goal to get me this summer.

I don't know why.

But suddenly, it feels good.

It feels fucking good to be pursued like this, after being the one who was on the giving end of unrequited affection for so long.

She wants me.

Through the glass, Nora's eyes meet mine and holds my gaze. She swims on her belly for a while, her eyes just above the surface of the water, never looking away from my own.

She splashes and kicks at me, flipping onto her back.

Her tits bob above the water, her nipples pointed to the sun.

My dick twitches again.

And then when she's finally done showing off for me, she emerges from the water, dripping wet and bathed in sunlight.

She's sexy as hell.

And she knows it.

She strides back across the lawn, watching me every step of the way. She climbs the back steps, crosses the kitchen, and pauses in front of me, dripping on my feet.

"I'm cold," she murmurs into my ear, leaning up on her tiptoes. She is. Her cold skin grazes against me, bleeding through my shirt, as her tits press into my chest. Her nipples are hard enough to cut glass and my hands ache to slide along her skin, over her hips, down to where I'd grip her ass and...

I grit my teeth.

"Then you should get dressed," I tell her calmly, bending to pick up the towel she'd discarded earlier and handing it to her. I make no move to touch her, regardless of how much my traitorous fingers want to slip in between her legs and...

I grit my teeth again.

She sees my jaw flex and grins victoriously.

She knows that she won the game she was playing... that she made me want her.

I don't bother telling her that I wanted her already.

Instead, I just meet her gaze and hold it, until she steps back and walks away.

This time, instead of staring at her bare ass, I focus on the black words tattooed on her shoulder blade. I saw them earlier, but I was too distracted to read them, even though they make me curious.

Nora isn't the type of girl I would've figured for a tattoo.

She's refined, buttoned-up, classy.

But even still, she has black words tattooed on her shoulder blade, with a small elegant anchor. *Fluctuat nec mergitur.*

It's Latin. What does it mean?

I pull my phone out of my pocket and punch the words into a search engine.

A result is immediately returned.

She is tossed by the waves, but she does not sink.

It has meaning. It's symbolic. The ink is stark black and the tattoo looks new.

It's a reminder to her... to stay strong. To be resolute. To never sink no matter what.

My eyes narrow as I remember the text on her phone.

I want your word. And I want you to keep it.

I know where you are.

Something happened to her. Something she doesn't want to talk about, something that she's scared of, something that involves this William person.

I've seen the fear in her eyes a couple of different times, but she always covers it up.

I've seen that kind of fear before, in the eyes of women in Afghanistan. In the eyes of women who had been beaten and abused and raped.

My stomach clenches at the memory, but also for Nora.

Someone has hurt her.

But that someone won't do it again, not while she's here on my watch.

Of that, I am certain.

Resolutely, I make my way back out to the living room and drop into the chair by the windows. I wait while Nora gets dressed, and ponder our situation the whole time.

We're like two prize fighters, circling around a ring, each waiting for the other one to pounce.

We've both got secrets that we don't want the other to know.

It's kind of ironic.

Nora finally emerges, clad in a t-shirt with no bra and short shorts. Her nipples poke through the thin material and the corners of her mouth twitch.

She knows exactly what she's wearing.

I smile at her.

"How was your swim?"

She smiles back.

Thrust and parry.

"It was refreshing. How was watching?"

I hold her gaze and smile again.

"It was refreshing."

Her grin widens.

"I forgot to get breakfast stuff for tomorrow. What would you like?"

You.

"Eggs," I suggest.

She nods. "Wise choice. I think I can manage eggs."

She grabs her purse.

I lift an eye-brow and glance at her chest again, at the way her bare tits strain against the t-shirt and her nipples poke against the fabric.

"Don't you want to put on a bra?"

I somehow manage to keep my voice level.

She grins angelically and leans down to whisper in my ear, her tits pressed against my shoulder.

"No. I want you thinking about my nipples while I'm gone. They taste like honey."

Jesus.

With that, she saunters away.

I swallow hard.

Cold fish. Cold fish. Cold fish.

Cold.

Fucking.

Dead.

Fish.

Somehow, I doubt that even the thoughts of cold dead fish are going to help me this summer.

Chapter Seven

Brand

There's nothing to do out here but stew in the idea that I'm trapped in Angel Bay. There's barely a cell signal, I can't get around and I can't drive yet.

Perfect.

Oh, and add to that that the girl who is sharing my cottage wants to have strings-free sex with me and for some reason, I turned her down.

What the fuck is wrong with me? I'm just going to blame it on the pain pills. They've addled my brain.

With a groan, I push myself out of the chair I'm in and hobble toward the door, my crutches scraping on the floor.

"Where are you going?" Nora asks curiously as she walks from the laundry room to the living rom with a load of fresh laundry in her arms.

"Fishing."

Nora starts to laugh until she sees that I'm serious.

"Fishing?"

I nod. "I can't do anything else. But I can sure as hell sit on a pier."

Nora stares at me for a second, then sits the laundry basket down, trailing behind me.

I pause and look at her. "Where are you going?"

She grins up at me. "Fishing. I've never been."

I raise an eyebrow. "You've lived in Angel Bay every summer of your life and you've never been fishing?"

She shakes her head emphatically. "Nope. There was no one to take me. My father would rather die than bait a hook, it held no interest for my mother, and our gardener Julian liked to go alone. He did all kinds of other stuff with me, but fishing was his quiet time. So... no. I've never been."

"That seems like a travesty," I tell her as I turn back around. I eye the distance from here to the shed outside, to the edge of the pier. It seems like a hundred fucking miles with these crutches.

"Well, then. End the madness for me," she chirps cheerfully by my side. "Actually, I'll meet you out there. I'm going to get a suit on."

"Take your time."

Because it will take me a hundred years to get situated.

Fuck.

She does take her time. Because it takes me twenty minutes to hobble to the shed, find a couple of poles and a bait-box and then drag all of that stuff to the end of the pier. All while on crutches.

I feel quite accomplished as I drop it all, then sit on the edge, carefully dangling my feet over the board pier. It hurts to bend my knee, of course, but not as much as it did yesterday.

That's progress, damn it.

I'm baiting a hook with a lure when Nora comes prancing down the pier in a pair of heels and a bikini so tiny it might as well not be there. I stifle a groan as she leans down next to me, making sure to stick her ass out as she does.

Her ass is perfectly rounded.

I look away as I cast my line.

Cold fish. Cold fish in the lake. Cold fish, cold fish.

"Want a pole?" I ask her, watching my bobber float on the surface of the water. Nora chuckles.

"Yes. Didn't I make that clear last night?"

I roll my eyes. "Are you always like this?"

She picks up the pole next to me, fiddling with it. "Like what?"

"So. Uh. Desperate."

She sucks in a breath and turns to me, indignation spitting from her eyes. I almost laugh.

"I'm not desperate," she announces, sticking her nose in the air as she further tangles the line on her pole. Annoyed, she tosses it down. "That's broken."

I can't help but laugh as I pick it up and untangle it for her, handing it back. "Don't mess with that part," I point at the line. "Hold this button down, then release it as you cast it. Like this."

I demonstrate.

"And you're acting desperate. A woman like you doesn't need to beg someone to fuck her."

My tone is probably harsher than it needed to be because I can practically see her flinch.

"I'm not desperate," she repeats, softer this time. "I just... I know what I want. And I only have a limited time to get it. That makes me driven, not desperate."

I stare at her, at the way the sun is already flushing her cheeks, at the strange look in her eyes... vulnerable, but determined. And I can't help but wonder once again, why she wants me so much.

I'm not stupid. I know I'm not lacking in female attention. But a girl like Nora can have literally anyone she wants. And girls like that don't usually throw themselves at someone....because they think they're above that.

It mystifies me.

We're quiet for a while, surrounded by the scent of the hot wooden boards, the lake water, the sunshine.

But it doesn't take long for Nora to get antsy, and I can see why her gardener wanted to be alone to fish.   She chatters, and I sigh.

"You know, when you talk, you scare away the fish," I finally tell her.

She glares up at me.

"You're not catching anything anyway."

I sigh again. "It takes time. And patience."

She falls silent for just a minute, then my mouth falls open as she unties her bikini top.

"What the hell are you doing?" I blurt as she drops her top on the pier and sits topless in the broad daylight.

"I don't want lines," she shrugs. "There's no one out here anyway. This is a private pier."   She turns her back to me, and thrusts a plastic bottle over her shoulder.   "Put some sunscreen on my back, would you? It's a curse of being a ginger, I burn easily."

You've got to be fucking kidding me.

It's the oldest trick in the book. A chick asks you to put lotion on them at the beach in order to get attention.

But still, I sit staring at her bare back, at the expanse of creamy white flesh facing me, and before I know it, I'm grabbing the bottle of sunscreen and dumping some in my hand.

My fingers glide over her soft skin, smoothing the lotion over her slender body, skimming over her shoulders, the friction between our skin warming my hand.

My groin reacts to such a simple act, tightening, constricting, *noticing*.

Hell.

Nora turns with a smile.

"Now my front?"

She thrusts her chest out and her perky tits are in my face, perfect, young and lush. My dick is rock hard by this point.

"You can do your own front," I growl. "In fact, put your suit back on. You're not a stripper. You don't know if someone will show up here."

She cocks her head and keeps her chest thrust proudly out. "No one will. It's just you and me."

"For now," I tell her firmly. "But you never know. Stop acting like a bar whore and put your clothes on."

The words come out before I can stop it, a reaction to my own frustration, to my own gut reaction at her nakedness.

Her face falls and her eyes shutter closed, she's expressionless now, sullen as she reaches for her top.

"I didn't realize I was so offensive," she mutters. "I'm sorry. I'll just leave you alone out here."

She stalks away and I can hear her heels clicking on the pier with every step she takes, as she gets further and further away.

I feel awful for crushing her. And I did crush her. I saw it in her eyes before she guarded them. I saw it in the way her shoulders fell, the way she sucked in her breath at my words.

I don't know why I said what I said... except that I want her to find her dignity.

I know, somehow I know, that this isn't really Nora. Nora Greene doesn't act like this. So why she feels the need to act like a bar whore around me, I have no fucking clue.

All it's doing is making it harder on me. Harder to not take her up on her proposition.

With a start, I realize that's exactly what she's doing. She's making it harder on me to say no.

With a groan, I roll my eyes and cast my line again.

Fuck. Like I need that. I'm having a hard enough time saying no already.

***

Nora

Fuck him.

I don't need this shit.

I storm into my room and yank a t-shirt and yoga capris out of a drawer. I'm here to help him, out of the goodness of my heart, and he wants to treat me like a common whore?

What the hell?

What is wrong with him that he won't just take me up on my offer? Jesus.

And there was no need to be so mean.

His words made my hands shake... I'm not a whore.

I pull on my clothes and twist my hair into a bun at my neck. I'm just starting to throw my clothes back into my bag, when I catch sight of a picture sitting next ot the lamp... an old photograph, framed in sea shells.

It's Brand, Gabe and Jacey.

Brand and Gabe must be around twelve, which means Jacey is just a bit younger. They're tanned and smiling and lying on the beach with popsicles. Their mouths are red and Jacey's got her arms wrapped around Brand's waist.

Something about that picture gives me pause, and makes me stop packing.

Being only twelve, I'm sure Brand hadn't even begun to notice Jacey yet... she was a couple of years younger after all. But it does show that even way back then, Jacey was clinging to Brand.

It started so long ago.

It makes me seethe, because I don't know Jacey, but I know girls like her.

She started clinging to him, making him feel important to her, reeling him in, going to him for advice, growing closer and closer. She kept him on the hook just in case she ever decided she wanted him... but then she never did, because he was like her 'brother.'

And Brand never saw it coming, because he's such a good guy. He never knew he was getting played, getting strung along.

Then when he bared his heart to her, she probably crushed it.

I stare at the picture, at the blonde little girl with her arms wrapped around Brand, and I can't help but hate just a bit. She hurt him, and now he's distant from every other woman as he protects himself from that happening again.

He hasn't said, but I know that's what he's doing.

All because of her.

In the picture, he's young and innocent. He's laughing at Gabe, still oblivious to the hooks Jacey would cast into him a bit later.

It twinges at my heart and I stop packing.

Because it reminds me that *he's so fucking good.* As I look at his boyish face in the picture, all I can see is teenage Brand, the boy who picked me out of the dirt and cleaned me off, all at the risk of getting in trouble. The sexy boy who grew into a sexy man, a man who fought hard for his country, a man who loved a woman he couldn't have.

Even though he's hardened and cautious now, he's still *good.*

That's why he doesn't want me throwing myself at him, lowering myself to begging. He doesn't want it that way.

It's been so long since I've been around a good man, I didn't even think about that.

I put my clothes away.

I head out to the living room and fold the towels in the basket, all the while watching out the window.

Brand grows sweaty and takes off his shirt.

The sun beats down on his shoulders and back, tanning him even more. I literally ache to go out there and smooth sunscreen over his shoulders, running my hands over that rippled muscle, running my fingers over those fucking words.

I stand on a wall to protect what is mine.

I swallow hard.

The sun glints on his honey-blond hair, and a sheen of sweat appears on his forehead. He stretches, and leans back once again, his muscles flexing with every movement.

His pole twitches, and he grabs it, reeling it in.

He pops a fish off the end of the line, then drops it into a bucket next to him.

I smile because he looks so satisfied.

He stretches one more time, then slowly climbs to his feet, careful not to twist his injured knee.

He grabs the bucket and dumps it out into the lake… and I see two other fish fall back into the water and I'm shocked. Why would he sit out there in the sun if he was only going to throw the fish back?

I ask him as much when he finally emerges in the house a few minutes later.

He glances up at me, his hair damp from the heat.

"Because I can clean them, but I doubt you know how to cook them. So why should I kill them for no reason?"

He limps past me, headed for the shower, and his simple answer warms my belly.

He didn't want to kill helpless creatures for no reason.

This big, strong solider who had to kill people in combat has a kind enough heart that he doesn't want to kill fish if he doesn't plan on eating them.

If possible, I'm even more infatuated with this man.

Chapter Eight

Nora

I manage to make scrambled eggs for the third night without burning them. I feel like I've conquered the world once again as I slide the steaming mass onto a plate and push it toward Brand across the kitchen table.

He purposely keeps his eyes firmly planted everywhere but the front of my shirt.

I feel like a wanton hussy as I remember how until today, every time I leaned forward, I made sure to push my boobs out, making my nipples strain even further against my shirt. .

Ugh.

He must think I'm such a slut, which is exactly the opposite of what I am, or what I want him to think.

God, I'm so ridiculous.

"Eat up," I tell him. "I think it's even edible."

Brand grins and digs in, his large fingers wrapped around his fork as he shovels the eggs into his mouth. He nods.

"Not bad, Greene. I think you've mastered eggs."

I'm in the middle of thinking of a smart comeback when my phone rings. Ice immediately runs down my spine, because every time my phone rings now, I assume it's William.

But this time, my father's name is on the screen.

The ice remains firmly planted in my back, stacked neatly between my vertebrae.

"I'm sorry," I murmur to Brand as I grab the phone. "I've got to take this."

He nods, his eyes trained curiously on my face.

I take the phone outside, where I pace in the yard.

"Hi dad,' I answer.

My father doesn't bother with niceties or even a hello.

"William tells me you're not returning his calls," he says brusquely. My spine straightens even more.

"I don't have anything to say to him," I say through my teeth.

My father sighs, a razor sharp sound.

"Nora, I don't have to remind you. He owns fifty percent of Greene Corp. He and I have to unanimously approve any new ventures. I need him to see things my way. *Our* way. That means we have to keep him happy. He's a difficult person, but he likes you. Use that."

I suck in my breath. "He likes me? He more than likes me. You know what he did. I won't let him do that again, dad. I won't. Nothing is worth that."

"*This* is worth that, Nora," my dad answers coldly. "This is your job, just like it is mine and your brother's."

It might be my job, but my job description is decidedly different than my father's or Nate's.

"How can you ask this of me?" I whisper. "I don't understand. I'm your daughter."

Silence.

Then my father strikes, using his words as his weapons.

"Nora, stop being weak. You're a Greene. Act like it. Do what it takes. Do you think I've always enjoyed the things I've had to do? I don't give a fuck if you enjoy it. I don't give a fuck if you hate it. But you *will do* what it takes to make him happy and keep him on our side. You know damn well that the deal with the city of Chicago is riding on his approval. You will not fuck it up. Got it?"

I'm numb as I listen to my father's words, the words that condemn me into basically selling my soul, my decency and my body for the sake of the company. He's commanding me to do it. His own daughter. Most fathers do everything they can to protect their daughters. Not mine.

Because I'm silent, my father prods me.

"Do we have an understanding?"

I'm still silent because honestly, I can't force myself to speak. My mind is a flurry of words and sensations and horror and I just can't manage to move my lips.

You're a Greene, Nora. Act like it.

I shudder as I think about the last time my father had said those words to me. It was after the 'incident'. The mere memory of the 'incident' makes me need to shower and without another word, I hang up on my father.

I rush back in the house and breeze past Brand, who is cleaning off the table.

"I saved your plate," he starts to tell me, but I hold up my hand.

"I need a shower," I call over my shoulder. He's frozen in place staring at me, a look of utter shock on his handsome face.

I'm aware that I look like a crazy person. But I've got to get the handprints off of me. They might be only memories, but I can still feel each one.

I let the hot water scald my back, running over my face and my hips. I let it wash away my doubts and my fear and my memories.

It's when I'm in the shower, and only when I'm in the shower, that I feel truly clean. I scrub myself until my skin feels red and raw, until the handprints have been scalded off.

As the water pours over me, I do what I always have to do when this happens. I focus on any possible thing to turn my mind away from the nightmare of that night, to forget the invisible hands on my body.

Today, it helps to focus on Brand.

Brand's smile, Brand's strength. The ornery way his eyes twinkle. His goodness.

His goodness.

I sigh again as I towel off. Brand is far too good for me.

Which is funny, because even as I feel tainted and unworthy because of….everything, I'm still acting like a hussy to get Brand to notice me. To get him to take me up on my no-strings offer for the summer.

Why am I doing this?

Brand's right. It's so not me.

But I'm desperate, just for a few weeks, to see if I can lose myself in Brand. To see if his goodness can eclipse the part of me that is so irrevocably damaged, just for a little while. He's the only one good enough to do it.

I'm selfish, I know. I'm selfish for being willing to let him put himself in someone's body who is so… used.

I shudder, and I can't hold the nausea back any more.

I lunge for the toilet and hang my head in it, emptying my stomach. I retch and retch and then there are cool hands on my back, and fingers lifting my hair away from my face and holding it back.

"It's okay," Brand tells me quietly, stroking my back with his rough hands. "It's okay."

He has no idea that I need comforting. I don't know why I'm not humiliated that he's here as I'm vomiting, but it seems perfectly right.

He's all I want.

When he's here, everything is okay.

I wipe my mouth and fall back against him, perfectly aware that I'm naked, but not willing to try and use it to my advantage.

Brand pulls me to my feet, and holds me up.

"Was it something you ate?" he asks gently.

Yeah. A wrinkled penis that was shoved in my mouth months ago.

I shake my head. "I don't know. I'm just going to brush my teeth and go to bed early."

"Okay. Call if you need me," Brand tells me again, concern in his husky voice. I can't bring myself to even look at him, because I'm afraid that if I do, he'll see what I am. He'll know what I did. He'll know that I wasn't strong enough to stop it.

"Okay."

I listen to the creak of Brand's crutches as he walks out, then I brush my teeth and wash my face.

My fingers still shake. The sick feeling lingers.

I'm alone. I'm so fucking alone.

I know that Brand is in the other room, and I know that even if miracle of miracles, I manage to make him want me this summer, he'd never want me if he knew what I've done. He'd never want me, and I could never take seeing the repulsion on his face if he ever found out.

He can never find out.

I wouldn't be able to take the rejection.

I reach for the bottle of sleeping pills sitting on my nightstand. I haven't been able to sleep without them for months, ever since *it* happened. While I hesitate to put anything chemical in my body now, anything mind-altering, I know that if I don't take these blessed little pills, I'll never sleep again.

I'll never sleep again because I'm afraid of the shadows, and of what they might bring. I have good reason.

I gulp it down, and lean back, waiting for sweet oblivion. It comes rather quickly and I fall asleep breathing in the sweet lavender smell of my pillow.

Unfortunately, as sometimes happens, the pills also bring vivid dreams, or in this case, nightmares.

Memories.

The problem is, even though I know they're nightmares, it's hard to wake up. It's like I'm tied to the bed, like I once was, unable to move.

My body writhes as I try to get away.

Hands.

Hot breath.

Straps.

Slaps.

Pinches.

Sucks.

Bites.

Pain.

Skin rubbing mine.

I'm too weak to move.

I can't move.

I can't breathe.

I can't breathe.

I can't breathe.

I wake up screaming.

And as I sit up and open my eyes, I see the only thing that makes me feel safe.

Brand.

Chapter Nine

Brand

Nora's shrill screams had woken me from a dead slumber. I'd leaped from bed and twisted my knee in the process, but it sounded like the hounds of hell were literally at her tail from the way she was screaming.

But now, I see she was only dreaming.

Her face is devoid of all color, so pale it almost looks silver as she sits in the light of the moon. Her hands are twisted in the sheets so tightly that her knuckles are white.

She looks up and sees me, and relief floods her face.

"Brand," she breathes.

She's limp and still and I fight the urge to cross the room and pull her to me. She seems so helpless and alone.

"Is everything all right?" I say instead, remaining in the doorway.

She nods. "I'm sorry if I woke you. I just...had a bad dream."

I know all about bad dreams.

I clear my throat, very aware that Nora is naked in her sheets. She doesn't seem to even notice, so I know that her fear right now is very real.

"Okay. I just wanted to make sure."

I turn to leave, but her voice stops me.

"Wait."

I turn back and her face is pensive.

"Can you stay?"

She's naked.

"Uh. I don't think that's a good idea."

Because she's naked and this is not a smart thing.

She hardly lets me finish before she interrupts.

"Please. I don't want to be alone."

The panic I see in her blue eyes does me in and I sigh.

"Okay."

There's no other place in this small bedroom to sit other than the bed. So Nora slides over a bit, and I drop onto the other side of the bed. I stay on top of the covers.

"Thank you."

Nora's voice is small as she huddles back down into the bed. I glance down and find that only her nose is sticking out, and a few tendrils of dark red hair. Her fingers are still tightly wound around the sheets.

I smile in the dark, then reach over and pry her fingers loose, straightening them out, forcing her to relax her grip.

Her eyes open.

"What are you afraid of?" I ask her quietly, staring into them.

She blinks.

"Everything," she sighs, surprising me.

The dark almost seems suffocating, and against my better judgment, I close my hand over hers, holding her fingers.

"Don't be," I tell her. "I'm here now."

She sucks in her breath, I hear it. And I regret my words. I don't want her to grow dependent on me. We're only here a short time. I can't get sucked in. I won't let it be another situation like the one with Jacey.

Nora reaches for me, and I tense. It's visible.

She stares at me through the dark, her eyes narrowing.

"What are *you* afraid of?"

"Nothing," I answer out of habit. She narrows her eyes more.

"Let me ask that again. What are *you* afraid of?"

"This," I finally answer.

Nora sucks her breath in again. "Why?"

I shake my head. "Because nothing good can come of it. We're only here for a few weeks."

Nora's lips curve into a slow smile. "Brand, trust me. A whole lot of good can come from it."

She reaches for me, her slender arms curving around my neck, pulling my face down to hers.

And while I know I should push her away, I should get up and leave, I don't.

Her lips taste sweet as they press to mine. I slide my hands up her warm back and pull her to me, crushing her against my bare chest. Our combined warmth ignites and her tongue slides into my mouth.

"I need you, Brand," she breathes. "I need you."

She slides her hand down my chest until she finds my hardness and I hear the rush of air as her breath rushes over her lips.

Her cool fingers grasp me, and I know that it's over. Logical thought escapes me and all I can focus on is the friction of her hand stroking my cock.

Smart or not, I'm burying myself in her tight little body tonight.

The chips can fall where they may.

***

Nora

Sweet Mary.

He's enormous.

And hard.

And it's all for me.

These are my thoughts as I slide my fingers up and down his shaft. With each touch, he gets harder, if that's even possible. He's as hard as steel.

I can't believe he's giving in.

His warmth is delicious. His hard chest pressed against mine...gah.

And then his fingers find me. He slides them into my wetness and he groans into my ear.

"Jesus, you're so wet already."

"I want you," I tell him simply. "I've always wanted you."

He groans again, his fingers sliding in and out, faster, then slow, then fast.

My fantasy is coming true tonight.

He lowers his head and pulls a sensitive nipple into his mouth, licking at first, then sucking. I throw my head back, my fingers wrapped in his hair. He sucks harder, then he pulls away.

"Don't stop," I tell him. "Please."

He sucks the other nipple. "I want them to match."

I smile, but out of the blue, as Brand hovers above me, the old panicky feeling comes back and I see William's face instead of Brand.

I'm frozen for a minute, the breath caught in my throat, as I fight to get past it.

This is Brand.

This is Brand.

He'll never hurt you.

Brand notices my tight arms and pulls away, even though his breathing is ragged.

"Are you ok?"

I nod, gulping air.

I want this.

Yes.

He'll make me good for just a while. I need this.

"I need you," I tell him again, forcing myself to relax.

He pulls me close, so close I can hear his heart against my ear. With one strong hand splayed against my back, he reaches the other around and strokes me with it.

Gah.

He knows just what to do… just where to touch me to get my body to sing. To make me forget the shame of William…just for a little while.

I arch against him.

"I want you inside of me," I pant. "Now."

I've waited years for this.

"Patience," Brand murmurs into my ear, his breath hot. He lowers his head, sucking my breasts again, gently, then harder. He moves his hand in circles, fast, then faster. He works me up, over the cresting waves, building, building, building.

I can't breathe now and I rock my hips against him.

He's gentle, yet firm, strong, yet careful. He's a beautiful contradiction… and exactly what I need

I need him.

I need him.

I can't breathe.

Then the world explodes in a bright shattering of whites and blues and reds.

I ride the orgasm, rocking against the palm of Brand's hand until the last waves of it have passed. Then I fall limply against him, his strength absorbing my weakness.

He lifts my chin with his finger, then buries his tongue in my mouth. Deep, deeper.

Then all of a sudden, in one fluid motion, he buries his cock in me, sliding it deep within me.

I groan and tilt my hips.

I want all of him.

All.

Of.

Him.

Make me good, Brand.

I want to absorb him, to take his goodness and cover myself with it. Nothing can hurt me when he's with me. When he's inside of me, he takes away the shame.

"God, you feel good," Brand groans as he moves inside of me. I cling to him, like a drowning person to a raft.

Each time he slides into me, a wave of pleasure erupts... building, building, building. *Again.*

I come again without warning, in a haze of moans and whimpers. I throw my head back and let my body convulse with it, as Brand pauses and pulls my ribcage up to him, his lips finding my breasts once again.

Again.

Again.

He worships them again, one by one, his tongue laving my nipples, sucking on the sensitive flesh.

I want to die right here in his arms.

It would be a good way to die.

When I open my eyes, he's waiting to stare into them, poised above me like the avenging angel that he is.

His muscle flexes.

"I'm going to come in you," he tells me simply.

I nod. "I'm on the pill. It's okay. I've been tested... it's okay."

Brand nods and buries himself in me once again and I want to scream with it, with the way he fills me up. His hardness, my softness. It's perfect.

He's perfect.

"I want to feel you come," I tell him urgently, pulling him back into me. *Give me everything you have. I need to feel it.*

Brand rocks with me, holding me in his strong arms until he throws back his head and groans with his release.

I feel his cock quiver inside of me, contracting as he comes. He comes and comes and comes.

He relaxes against me, but doesn't let me go.

"What did we just do?" he finally whispers against my forehead, after minutes or hours have passed. Everything is a blur around me, but I don't care.

He sounds slightly dismayed, but I don't care about that, either.

Because I'm ecstatic.

"You just made my dreams come true," I answer. "The good ones," I clarify.

Brand shakes his head and rolls to the side, keeping me in his arms. "Was it everything you thought it would be?" he asks drily, with amusement.

I nod. "And more."

Now that I've been with him, it's not going to be enough. I know that. I'm always going to want him. Everyone else will just pale in comparison.

But as I burrow against his chest, a hard truth impales my heart.

I can't be with him long. I can't eclipse his good heart with my black one. I won't do it.

This summer is all I have.

No matter what.

Even though it will kill me to leave him.

Even though he's all I want.

I would never shackle him to someone like me.

Never.

I fall asleep listening to the steady cadence of his heart.

When I wake, the sunshine is streaming through my windows, and Brand is gone.

Chapter Ten

Brand

I stir the scrambled eggs in the pan, carefully balancing on my good foot as I twist around to pour a glass of orange juice, because I'd woken up guilty and unable to sleep.

So here I am making breakfast.

What did you do?

You're such a fucking idiot.

I ignore my inner voice, but it's a persistent asshole.

Nora isn't the kind of girl that you fuck around with and leave. And she's not the kind of girl who will want you. Not for real.

I'd like to punch my inner voice in the teeth.

I'm in a predicament now, because I listened to my cock last night instead of my head. With a sigh, I hobble with my crutch under one arm and Nora's breakfast in my other hand.

I poke my head around the corner to find that she's awake.

"Good morning," I tell her quietly. I hobble in and set the plate on her bed. "I thought you might be hungry."

She stretches like a sated cat.

"I am," she announces with a grin. "I depleted my energy stores last night." She flushes prettily, and picks up her plate.

"About last night..." I begin and sit on the edge of the bed. Nora looks up warily.

"You can't go back," she interrupts firmly. "The bullet has already left the gun. There's only one thing you can do now… take me up on my proposition."

I exhale.

"Nora, I meant what I said earlier. You're better than that. You're worth more than some 'proposition.'"

I don't know why I feel like I need to tell her that. She's Nora *Greene* for God's sake. She knows what she's worth.

She stares at me like I have two heads.

"As I told you earlier, you don't know what I'm worth. I do. I want you, Brand. I know we only have a few weeks but I want *every day* of those few weeks. You're here, I'm here. It's perfect."

I raise an eyebrow. "So you want me because it's convenient?"

She giggles and takes a drink of juice. "No, I want you because I want you. It's just nice that it's convenient."

"You're… something," I tell her, shaking my head. I don't know what to make of her.

She glances up, her eyes filled with laughter. "Good. That's better than nothing."

She takes a bite of eggs, then glances up at me.

"What should we do today?"

I shrug. "There's not much to do. We're stuck in a cottage in Angel Bay. Without cable."

Nora rolls her eyes. "Uh. There's plenty to do." She reaches up and slides her hand under my shirt, her fingertips grazing my nipple.

At just this minute, there's a heavy knock on the back door.

We look at each other.

"Saved by the bell," Nora grins. She gets out of bed and pulls on a robe. "Hold that thought. I'll get it."

I hear her pad down the hallway and I hobble behind her, feeling like a clumsy asshole with my fucking crutches.

When I reach the living room, Nora is already showing a man clad in a suit into the cottage.

"Brand, it's for you," she tells me hesitantly. "It's your dad's estate lawyer."

I study the guy... he's pasty, weaselish, and dressed in a tightly buttoned suit. He holds his hand out.

"I'm Todd Ansel," he tells me. "I represented your father and put his will together. Do you have a few minutes?"

"A *few*," I nod, making it clear that I only have a few. Nora has backed up now, and is lingering on the edge of the room.

"Do you need me to stay?" she asks me quietly. I shake my head.

"Nah. I've got this, but thank you."

She slips out and I stare at Todd. I don't offer him a seat.

"How can I help you?"

He clears his throat and sets his briefcase on the floor beside him. "I spoke with your mother and she indicated that you wanted to relinquish your rights to your inheritance and transfer it to her, instead."

I nod. "Yes."

Todd nods as well. "Yes, your father anticipated that you would do that. So he put a stipulation in his will."

I stare at him hesitantly. "A stipulation? My mother didn't mention that."

Todd nods again. "That's because she doesn't know."

I sigh heavily. Leave it to my father to do something fucked up, even in the end. "Well, what is it?"

Todd bends and sifts through his bag, coming up with a paper. He hands it to me, his weasel eyes focused on my reaction.

I don't give him one.

Instead, I scan the paper.

All I can focus on are the words, ***Brand must ring the bell.***

Shock slams into me, fast and hard, and anger clouds my vision.

What a fucker.

Todd clears his throat again. "I'm not sure what the purpose of this exercise is, but your father's wishes are clear. You must swim out to the large buoy in the bay and ring the bell, then swim back in. You must be un-assisted, you cannot use a boat or motorized device of any sort. You must swim on your own devices. If you don't complete this task, your inheritance will revert to the state. And you will not be given the key to the box your father left for you."

Through my anger, that snags my attention.

"A key?"

Todd raises an eyebrow. "You must not have tried to open the box yet. It's locked. I have the key. I'm instructed to give it to you only upon completion of the task."

Nora must've only lingered right outside the door, because she bursts back in now.

"What will happen if he doesn't do it?" she asks, her cheeks flushed.

Todd looks at her. "If Brand chooses not to complete the task, his inheritance will revert to the state, as I said. Bethany Killien will receive nothing. And it's my understanding that she does the books for Mr. Killien's mechanic business. It's likely that she will lose her job when the state sells the business."

"So my mother would have nothing," I clarify. "Not a house, not any money and she would lose her job."

Finally, Todd has the good graces to look uncomfortable. "Yes. I don't know what your father's motives were, but yes. Your mother would have nothing."

"Perhaps his mother *deserves* nothing," Nora snaps.

If I weren't already so annoyed with the situation, I would find her reaction amusing. She's so defensive on my behalf.

The lawyer shrugs. "I guess that's for Brand to decide." He looks at me. "You have thirty days from today to complete the task. I need to be present as a witness. Again, if you choose not to do it, the entire inheritance will default to the state."

"We understand that part," Nora says icily. "I'll show you out."

Todd picks up his briefcase and hands me his card.

"Call me when you're ready to take a cold dip in the lake."

He walks out. Nora closes the door behind him, then walks back to me.

"Why would your father do that?" she asks softly, her hand curled around my arm.

I shrug. "Who knows?"

But I know.

And Nora is fully aware of that. She stares at me knowingly.

"All right. I won't pry. For now. But what will you do?"

I shrug again, because this time I really don't know.

I don't know what I'll do. My mother probably doesn't deserve anything. But it's not in my character to let an old lady get kicked to the street. Even a cold-hearted old lady like my mother.

"I have to think about it," I finally answer. "It's not about swimming out to the buoy. It's about... what message I want to send to my mother."

Nora stares at me, her blue eyes understanding. "I don't blame you," she answers softly. "I wouldn't lift a finger for my father."

She turns around and walks away before I can ask her why.

Within a minute, she returns with her purse. "I'm going to run a quick errand, and then let's get out of here for the day," she suggests. "I've got cabin fever already."

"You don't have to stay here with me," I remind her. "There's no reason for both of us to be bored."

She rolls her eyes.

"After the line we crossed last night, there's no place I'd rather be."

She winks and I shake my head.

"Last night doesn't change anything."

She leans up and nips at my ear lobe.

"Last night changes *everything*."

With that, she walks out to her car and I can't help but watch her tight ass sway as she walks away.

With a sigh, I know that she's right.

It changed everything.

And honestly, I'm tired of fighting it.

Chapter Eleven

Nora

It takes forever to find a car rental place with a convertible, but I manage. Over an hour later, I pull back up to the cottage in a sporty red convertible with the top down.

Brand is reclining on the porch steps, his legs stretched out in front of him as he waits in the shade. His eyes widen a bit as I round the car and walk toward him.

"What did you do?"

I giggle. "Well, I didn't sell the Jag or anything. I rented this for the day. Let's drive around the lake with the wind in our hair, then have a picnic."

Brand raises an eyebrow. "Did you cook any part of the lunch?"

I roll my eyes. "No. It's already in the car, pre-bought. All I need is you now."

The corners of his mouth twitch, but he doesn't argue. He just picks up his crutches and heads toward the car. His bulging biceps flex as he takes each step.

I gulp, remembering how they'd flexed as he'd balanced above me last night, how his skin had glistened in the moonlight, how he had groaned into my neck. Warmth gushes into my panties.

Gah.

Brand glances at me. "What?"

My cheeks are burning. And he noticed.

I shake my head. "Nothing. Are you ready?"

"Always." His lip twitches again. He drops into the car, and puts the crutches in the small back seat. "Ready."

I fasten my seatbelt and pull my hair into a quick ponytail, before I drive out of the driveway and down the road.

The breeze from the lake is fresh and clean this morning, blowing gently against our faces. The sun gleams on the top of the water and the temperature is absolutely perfect.

I stick to roads that hug the lake, rather than drive on the highway. We leisurely drive, chatting about nothing and everything, as though we don't have anything more important to do at all, as though his dad wasn't conniving and hateful, as though he doesn't have that stupid will hanging over his head and I don't have a hateful job waiting for me at the end of the summer.

It's really nice.

Brand glances over at me. "Why did you go to law school?"

The question surprises me. "Why did you go to the Rangers?"

He shakes his head. "That's not the same thing. Being a Ranger suited me. Being a lawyer doesn't suit you."

My mouth drops open as I look at the road again. "Why do you say that?"

Brand shrugs. "Because you're not cold-hearted or ruthless. It's a strange occupation choice for you, that's all."

I feel my cheeks flush again, and I wish they wouldn't.

"You don't know me," I tell him firmly. "If the situation calls for it, I can do what it takes. My dad has drilled that into my head since I was a toddler. *Be a good Greene, Nora. Do what it takes.* It's worked out okay for me. I was valedictorian of my senior class, and then I graduated Stanford Law School with a perfect GPA."

"That's nice," Brand smirks. "We can put that on your gravestone after you work yourself into the ground."

I scowl. "What does that mean?"

Brand levels a gaze at me and I look away. "It means that there is more to life than striving to be someone you're not. I get that you want to please your dad. I saw him back in the day, back when I worked at the club. He's a...commanding person. Intimidating. I can see why you'd want to please him. But your life is your own."

I swallow hard, because a lump suddenly formed in my throat. "And now you're an expert?"

Brand shakes his head and looks toward the lake. "Nope. I'm just observant."

I take a deep breath. *I've got to change the subject.*

"Well, then, observe this."

I slide my right hand along his inner thigh, and his athletic shorts that he's been wearing because of his knee brace give me easy access. I slip my fingers under the hem and up along his thigh, my fingers grazing his bare skin.

I hear his breath suck in.

I feel the velvety skin beneath my fingers.

I feel my pulse bounding right out of my veins.

Warmth floods my panties again.

This man is like crack to me.

For real.

I stroke his thigh, enjoying his quick breaths.

He doesn't stop me. I feel his hardness, and the way he engorges even more, growing harder and harder by the moment. I feel his dick grow against the back of my hand.

I stroke it lightly with my knuckles.

He takes a breath.

I exhale.

"It's time for lunch," I announce shakily, withdrawing my hand.

I turn onto a little road that leads to a look-out on the top of a bluff. From here, there's a perfect view of the lake. And there's no one else in sight. It's secluded and perfect.

I put the car in Park, then turn to Brand.

"I want your tongue in my mouth. Right now."

I'm imperative and bossy.

His mouth curls up.

But he reaches for me, his strong arms pulling me onto his lap.

His tongue plunges into my mouth, his lips firm and soft. He tastes like mint and man. My fingers splay on his chest, relishing the hardness beneath my fingers.

He kisses me breathless.

When he pulls away, I'm shaky.

He cocks an eyebrow.

"Again?"

I nod, because I'm a wanton hussy.

Brand smiles, like the sun, and grabs me again. He grips the base of my neck with one strong hand and pulls my face to his own.

I like his power. I like his strength.

Because I know he'd never use it on me.

I pull away and glance up into his ocean blue eyes. "Why are you doing this? I thought you said that it wasn't going to happen again?"

Brand's eyes cloud for a minute, then clear. He shrugs. "You're an adult. You know what you want. And I'm an adult. I know what *I* want."

He stares at me with his blue, blue eyes, his gaze so intense that it takes my breath away.

"I'll be good for you," I promise. "This summer, you're going to wonder what you ever did before me."

Brand's eyes cloud again, but he doesn't say anything. He just pulls me back to his mouth.

"Prove it," he growls against my lips.

I pop my head up and look around. No one is in sight.

With an impish grin, I pull at Brand's shorts.

"What are you doing?" he asks calmly, his eyebrow cocked. God, I love it when he does that. So cocky, so sexy. Is there anything sexier than Brand Killien on the face of the planet?

"You get three guesses," I tell him as I pull his shorts down to his knees and lean over him. I trail my tongue from the base of his dick to the tip. I glance up at him, my eyes locked with his as I trace a circle around the head of his cock. "What's your first guess?"

He swallows hard, then leans his head against the seat, closing his eyes as my mouth closes around the head of his dick.

"Jesus," he mutters, as I stroke the length of him as I suck.

For just one split moment, an ugly memory erupts in my head, one of a wrinkled penis and fetid breath. I cringe, and grip Brand's dick harder than necessary. His eyes open.

"Sorry," I mumble against the skin of his dick. I soften my grip and lick him again.

This is Brand. This is Brand. This is Brand.

He's brave and good and true. He would never hurt me.

I suck.

He swallows.

I glide my hand along his length, and cup his balls.

He swallows again.

I marvel at his hardness. I inhale his scent. I lick the velvet tip.

He grips my back.

"I want to be inside you," he murmurs, soft and husky.

"Not yet," I tell him.

I want to taste him. I want his goodness inside of me. I want to swallow it. Everything about him is just so fucking *good.* I want to absorb it in every way that I can.

I bob my head faster, my hand quickening its pace.

Brand groans again, his head falling back against the seat.

"I'm going to come," he warns me, his voice stilted.

I move faster and then I pull on his balls.

Give it to me.

He comes in my mouth, spurting hotly, his dick pulsing.

I suck it all in, swallowing, swallowing.

I lick him clean.

When I sit up, I smooth my hair back into place, as though I'd simply been out for a walk in the breeze.

"You ready for lunch?" I ask casually.

Brand smiles with his eyes closed.

"Maybe I'll take a nap first."

I punch him lightly on the arm. "Not even. You've got to regain your strength. I've got work for you to do in a while."

He opens one eye now, staring at me lazily. "Oh?"

I nod. "Yep. Let's go, Killien."

We take the picnic basket to the table on the lookout, and sit chewing on our sandwiches in the sun. In front of us, the lake glistens and crashes against the shore.

"I love it here," I tell him.

He looks at me in surprise. "I thought you said you hated it?"

I shake my head. "No. I just hate being at my parents' house."

He takes a bite. "Then why are you? You're an adult. You can do what you want."

Tightness pulls at my chest, the way it always does when I think about it.

"It's not that simple," I tell him. "I wish it were."

Brand falls silent and we eat.

When we're finished, I throw the trash away, then walk back to him, sliding up between his legs.

I stare into his gorgeous face.

"I don't know what changed your mind," I announce to him. "I know you were dead-set against being with me. But I don't care what it was. All I care about is the fact that you're in front of me right now. And you're mine for the summer."

I announce it like I'm staking claim, because I am.

And then I pull him to me, inhaling his scent right before I kiss him as deep as I can. I push my body into his, my hips into his. My tongue tangling with his. My body and his body.

Nora and Brand, forever and ever and ever.

Or at least, until the end of the summer.

Until I have to let him go before I taint him.

Glancing around, I find that there's still no one in sight.

An evil thought comes to me and I grin.

"You recovered yet?"

Brand raises an eyebrow, but doesn't have time to answer before I pull his shorts down a bit.

He yanks backward, staring at me in shock. But I don't give him time to process it. I drop my shorts, then sit immediately on his lap, without pause or foreplay.

I slide down the length of his already hard dick, my softness and warmth enveloping him.

"Jesus," Brand sighs again. I smile against his neck as I cling to him.

"You're going to come in me this time," I tell him softly.

"Yes, m'am," he answers huskily, lifting my hips with his hands as we rock together. I love the way his hands can span my waist. I love the way he makes me feel small and delicate and feminine. I love the way he fills me up.

I sigh into his mouth as his tongue invades mine.

We're in the middle of broad daylight and neither one of us cares.

We rock together until Brand finally throws his head back with his release.

And then he holds me close to his chest, while we both regain our bearings.

Slowly, the world comes back into focus and I glance up at him.

"See? You're not going to know what you did before me."

He closes his eyes in the sun and suddenly my own words scare me.

Because maybe I won't either.

Chapter Twelve

Brand

I'm an asshole.

I'm an asshole.

I'm an asshole.

That's all I can think as we drive back toward the cottage, with the radio up and the wind in our hair.

It's a perfect day, and I just fucked Nora Greene in the middle of broad daylight, after basically agreeing to a summer fling.

What the fuck am I doing?

Nora chooses this moment to reach over and grab my hand, holding it tightly while she drives. She doesn't look at me, she just gazes at the road and then the lake, then the road again.

Her red hair gleams under the sun, her skin luminous and creamy and my gut tightens.

What the fuck? Nothing good can come of this.

Why, then, does it feel so good?

Her hand feels perfectly at home inside of mine.

And you weren't arguing about your dick being inside of her mouth, either, my fucking devil side tells me persuasively.

I sigh.

This summer will probably kill me.

Or condemn me to hell.

At the moment, though, I don't care. Everyone around me has gotten where they are today not by thinking of other people, but by thinking of themselves. Putting themselves first. Maybe it's time I start.

Being with Nora feels good.

Isn't that enough of a reason?

The silence is comfortable and familiar as we drive to the rental car company and exchange cars and then head back for the cottage. We've managed to kill most of the day with driving, but it was nice.

Nora turns down Honeysuckle Drive. As we pass my mother's house, I grit my teeth, as I remember that her life is practically in my hands. Her life as she knows it, anyway. I sigh.

Fuck it.

She doesn't deserve my help.

But just as quickly as I have the thought, I think something else. No matter how much of a bitch she is, I don't want to give her the power to make me be someone I'm not. And I'm not an asshole.

Nora glances over at me.

"You know what I've recently decided?"

I shake my head. Of course I don't.

Nora stares straight ahead as she speaks.

"I've decided that I can't help how people treat me. All I can do is handle myself... and not let their actions reduce me. No matter what happens, I'm going to be me. They can't take that away."

What a curious thing to say. It's almost as if she can read my thoughts.

"That's very wise," I nod. "But easier in theory than practice."

Nora puts the car in park outside the cottage. "I know. Trust me. Wanna watch me practice?"

Puzzled, I start to ask what she's talking about, but then realize that another car is in the drive, a sleek black Mercedes.

Turning, I find Maxwell Greene sitting on the porch, waiting for us, dressed in an expensive suit and shiny loafers. He's as out of place on that porch as anyone I've ever seen. And from the expression on his face, he doesn't want to be here, either. I can see from the way he's looking at me that he doesn't approve of me.

At all.

I clench my jaw.

Fuck him.

I don't need anyone's approval.

I climb from the car and grab my crutches as Nora greets him.

"Hi dad," she calls cheerfully, but the smile on her face is forced. I wonder why she hates him so much? Because it's clear to me that she does.

Her father scowls.

"What are you doing here, Nora?"

He doesn't even bother to greet her, as if she's too unimportant to waste his breath.

Nora flinches, but covers it up.

"As you know, Brand was injured when he was *saving my life*," she places emphasis on those words. "I'm here to help him while he's recovering. It's the least I can do."

As Nora's father rolls his eyes, I remember the day of the accident, and how I'd glanced behind me and saw him and his wife, talking to the EMTs. Nora's mother was anxious and hysterical, while Maxwell was as cool as he could be. Almost unconcerned.

What kind of father does that?

I stick out my hand. "I don't think we've officially ever met. Brand Killien."

Maxwell stares at my hand for a minute, almost in distaste, before he stiffly takes it.

"Maxwell Greene," he replies gruffly. He looks immediately away to Nora.

"It's time to come home. You're supposed to be relaxing this summer, getting ready for the Fall. And William is at our house. He's waiting to talk to you."

Nora instantly goes pale. The horror on her face is obvious and very, very revealing.

She opens her mouth, then closes it.

I step forward.

"I don't mean to intrude, but Nora promised me that she would take me to Physical Therapy this evening."

Her father barely glances at me. "Well, I guess you'll have to get someone else to do it. Nora, I'll meet you back at home."

You're welcome for saving your daughter's life, asshole.

He starts to walk toward his car.

Nora is frozen, but then she glances at me.

I nod. *Be strong, Nora. Don't let him control you.*

She looks into my eyes, searching for something, something I can't name. She must find it, because she squares her shoulders and takes a step.

"Actually, dad, I can't come home right now. I've got an obligation here. I gave my word, and I need to keep it. Isn't that how you raised me?"

Her voice starts out tremulous, but grows steadier. Maxwell stops in his tracks, then turns slowly.

I can see the displeasure on his face, from the idea that his daughter dared to defy him.

There's a coldness in his eyes that is familiar to me. I used to see it in my own father.

He takes a step, and I move slightly in front of Nora.

I stare into his face.

If you want her, you'll come through me, asshole.

Humor fills his eyes.

"Are you going to do something, gimp?" Maxwell asks, his voice quiet and even. I smile at this. I could level this guy out with two gimpy legs and one hand tied behind my back. But I don't say that. I don't have to. He knows.

I stand my ground because actions speak louder than words.

Maxwell stares at his daughter, his gaze unyielding.

Finally, he turns.

"We'll discuss this later, Nora. Your mother is hosting a dinner on Friday. You'll be there."

Without even looking at us again, he gets into his car and drives away.

I hear Nora exhale from behind me.

I turn around and stare into her face. She's still pale, still shaky.

"Are you ok?"

She nods.

"Yeah. Thank you for... thank you."

I nod. "I don't like bullies."

"Me either," she murmurs. She stretches on her toes to get the house key and unlocks the door.

As we go in, she turns to me. "I think I have to go to my mother's dinner. Will you go with me?"

Her voice is strained, her eyes empty.

I immediately agree. "Of course."

"Thank you. I'm going to... take a shower. Are you ok out here for a while?"

"Of course."

I watch her walk away, her back stiff, her hands fisted at her sides.

She's in the shower for a long time.

The physical therapist comes and does his thirty minutes of PT with me before Nora finally emerges from the bathroom, steamy and clean.

"How did PT go?" she asks curiously as she steeps some tea in a china cup. I notice that her arms are red. She scrubbed them with force.

I shrug. "It's ok. I know what to expect. This isn't my first rodeo."

Nora sits in the chair next to me by the window.

"Was your leg really shattered before?"

"Pretty much. I think I've got more metal and screws in it than bone. But it's okay. I can walk, which is more than a lot of guys."

Without meaning to, I think of Mad Dog, my old colleague and friend, whose legs were blown off in front of me. He hadn't survived.

"This dinner," I change the subject. "What's it for?"

Nora shrugs. "I don't know. My father makes my mother host dinner parties for his business associates. It's hard to say who will be there or what this one is for."

I eye her carefully. "Will William be there?"

Nora tenses up, her hands gripping her china cup. "Probably."

I don't answer, although I'm even more assured now that I need to go with her to the dinner.

After a moment, Nora speaks. "What my dad said... about you being a gimp... don't listen to him. You're amazing. Your little pinky is more of a man than my father will ever be."

I have to smile at this. "It's okay. I don't usually let assholes influence the way I see myself."

She nods. "Good. Because sometimes I worry that you don't see yourself the way I do."

I cock my head, studying her in the dying light of the sun. "And how is that?"

She rolls her eyes. "Fishing for compliments?"

I shake my head. "Nope. Just trying to get your perspective."

"You're strong," she says firmly. "And brave and honorable and good. I've never met anyone like you. And I doubt I ever will again."

Her assessment takes my breath away.

The reverence in her voice takes me aback. She looks at me with adoration and I know I don't deserve it.

I start to shake my head, but she's already shaking her own.

"Don't bother," she tells me firmly. " I know what I know."

Whatever.

I pick up her hand and hold it, my rough thumb stroking hers. "Nora, I doubt I can live up to the fantasy that you have in your head. Of me, I mean. I'm just a guy. I do the best I can, but..."

She stares at me, impaling me with her blue gaze.

"Don't even try," she tells me softly. "It won't work. I see you for what you are, Brand. I only wish you could see it, too."

She stands and stretches, then takes her cup to the kitchen.

"I'm going to bed early," she tells me pointedly, staring at me with laser focus. "Do you want to join me?"

She turns and walks to the bedroom and without another word, I follow her.

She undresses with purpose, taking each article of clothing off slowly and carefully, her eyes locked with mine the entire time.

My dick stands to attention as her tits pop out of her bra.

"Come here," I tell her.

Obediently, she walks straight to me, her creamy skin hot beneath my fingers.

Dipping my head, I rake one of her strawberry nipples in my mouth. She throws her head back and digs her fingers through my hair.

"You do taste like honey," I tell her.

She smiles.

"Are you still hungry?" she asks wolfishly. I nod. "Always."

Chapter Thirteen

Nora

After Brand makes love to me for the third time today, he falls asleep in my arms.

I watch him sleep for the longest time, watching the way his face is so peaceful, the way he's vulnerable in a way that he never is when he's awake.

I wish I could stay like this forever with him.

Safe.

I swallow at the thought.

If only.

But I remember the look on my father's face earlier tonight. There will be hell to pay for that simple act of defiance.

I look down at Brand's sleeping face.

But it was worth it.

I fall asleep wrapped in his warm arms.

When I wake the next morning, I realize that it was the first night in months that I didn't have a nightmare.

Chapter Fourteen

Brand

Each day of the week passes peacefully, each night just as peaceful. Nora sleeps in my bed, curled into my side.

Each morning, she kisses me awake, her hair falling onto my face.

Today, after breakfast, I venture outside while she works from her laptop at the table. I make my way down to the gazebo that sits near the beach.

Dropping onto a bench, I stare at the lake.

More specifically, I stare at the large buoy floating a hundred yards out. The bell dings with the breeze, as the moss covered buoy tilts to and fro on the waves.

A shudder runs through me.

As I stare at it, I don't even see it anymore. Instead, in my head, I'm a boy again. And I still hear the dinging of that fucking bell.

I glance at the clock. Three a.m.

There's only one person who would come for me at three a.m.

I swallow hard, the acidic taste of bile rising in my throat. It won't go down, so I swallow harder, and the footsteps come closer.

My hands twist in the sheets, forming a fist....a fist that I know I won't use. I'm only twelve and he outweighs me by a hundred pounds.

I grit my teeth, flexing my jaw.

My bedroom door opens.

His shadow fills up my doorway, falling onto the floor. In

127

the blackness, his shadow resembles the monster he is.

"Get out here," he growls.

I force myself to succumb to numbness as I climb from bed. It's the only way I survive it… this… my life.

He grabs my arm, dragging me down the hall. Every other door remains closed, tight and dark. Like always, no one will come to my rescue.

I'm alone.

I'm used to it.

One foot after the other, I make the long walk. When the cold air hits my face, I don't even flinch. My bare feet burn from the snow. I still don't react.

All I do… all I can ever do… is brace myself for the pain.

It comes quickly.

My father backhands me hard, hard enough that I go flying into the frozen sand and I taste blood.

"Get up," my father snarls, alcohol on his breath. He's been at the bar, again. It's always when he comes home trashed that he drags me out here.

I stagger to my feet, and the world whirls around me. I see two of my father, before I blink and they blend back into one.

"Swim out and ring the bell," he demands.

I shake my head. "The lake is almost frozen," I tell him. "I can't."

My father's face contorts. "You're such a little chicken shit," he growls, backhanding the side of my head. I cup my ear with my hand and feel the blood as it trickles down my neck. It's warm.

"It's your fault she's dead," he tells me, his words as stark as the frozen lake. "And it should've been you."

He hits me again, and this time, I don't get up.

"A penny for your thoughts," Nora tells me softly, coming up from behind. She lays her hand on my shoulder and I glance up, trying to shake the old memories away.

"They aren't worth a penny," I tell her. And I mean it. She eyes me curiously, then stares out at the buoy.

"Thinking about your dad's will?"

No.

"Yeah," I lie.

She bites her lip as she stares into the distance. "Have you decided if you'll do it?"

I haven't even thought about it.

"I probably will," I tell her. "My mom wasn't the best mother, but even she deserves something for staying married to my father for so long."

Nora glances at me. "But do *you* deserve to have to be the one who gives it to her?"

I shrug. "I'm just going for a swim. No big deal."

She eyes me doubtfully. "But you hate to swim."

I nod. "Yeah, I do. But it won't kill me."

Nora can't see the way my palms go clammy at the thought. *Because damnit, Brand. Quit being a pussy.*

Nora smiles at me. "The UPS driver was just here. You got something from Gabe."

My tux. I'd called and asked Gabe's wife Maddy to ship it. They've got a key to my place.

"Ah," I tell her. "Good. It's Friday and I need something to wear."

Nora's face instantly clouds over and I regret mentioning it. But it *is* Friday. She's got to face it sometime, because the dinner is tonight.

"I'm sure your dad will be very happy to see me," I tell her drolly. She actually laughs at that.

"I'm sure," she agrees with a grin. "Don't be surprised if he hugs you."

"With his fist," I nod. She giggles again.

"He wouldn't have the balls," she tells me.

She's probably right. I could saw the fear hidden in his careful expression the other day.

We get up and walk back to the house, and as we cross the threshold of the living room, I can't help but look at the fucking wooden box that my dad left for me. It mocks me.

Nora follows my gaze.

"What do you think is in it?" she asks.

"I don't know," I tell her honestly. "I can't imagine."

"Do you want to know?"

"I don't know that, either," I'm honest again. "Part of me is curious. Part of me just wants to burn it without looking. I don't really care what he has to say to me."

Nora stops in her tracks and is perfectly still as she watches me. "What did he do to you?" she asks quietly.

I shake my head. "It's not worth talking about anymore. He's gone. And he took his hatefulness with him."

Nora takes a step, and puts her hand on my chest, feather-light, directly over my heart.

"He didn't take it all," she observes. "Part of it still lives on in here." She taps on my heart. "He put those scars there, Brand. Somehow. *You've* got to figure out how to get those scars off."

"I've heard vitamin E oil works," I tell her glibly, without acknowledging what she said. She rolls her eyes.

"I'm serious. Deal with it and put it to bed, Brand. Whatever he did to you, he can never do it again. Because he's gone."

"He is," I agree. "But so is my sister."

Why did I just say that? The words came out before I could stop them.

Nora's head snaps up.

"You have a sister?"

I opened this can of worms. With a sigh, I try and close it again.

"I did. She died a long time ago."

I try and walk past Nora, but she grabs my arm and stares up at me, her blue eyes so so serious, and so fucking perceptive.

"How did she die?" she asks quietly, never taking her eyes off of me.

I swallow.

"She drowned. Out in the lake."

"Oh my God," Nora breathes. "Did you see it happen? Is that why you don't like to swim?"

I look away, out at the water, at the sky, at the beach.

As I do, I can't help but remember that night.

"I was sleeping when it happened," I tell her woodenly. "My sister used to sleepwalk. They put a lock on her bedroom door on the outside, to lock her in so she couldn't hurt herself on the stairs. But that night, my father forgot to lock it when he tucked her in before he went to the bar."

Nora stares at me in horror.

"I don't know what to say," she finally says. "That's awful. Why does he want you to ring the bell?"

I shake my head and I hate to say the words. But I say them anyway, because they're the truth.

"Because sometimes, people can't blame themselves even when they know they're to blame. They just have to focus their anger on someone else, just to make it bearable."

Nora stares at me in confusion. "I don't understand. He blamed you? How in the world could it have been your fault?"

I swallow again, and again, trying to get the lump out of my throat. The fucking lump that forms whenever I think of Allison.

"My father was under the assumption that I should've heard her come out of her room in the middle of the night because my room was right across the hall. He thought that I *had* heard her and just chose not to follow her. See, back then, when I was little, I was scared of swimming in the lake. I wasn't scared of anything else... I wasn't scared of snakes or spiders or heights. But I was scared of the lake. I don't know why."

I stop speaking and stare out the window. In my head, it's that night. And it's black and terrible.

"He thought I was lying about not hearing her get up. He thought I was just too much of a chicken shit to follow her into the lake to save her."

I never knew that speaking the hateful words out loud would be so painful, so much like a scalpel to my throat.

Nora shakes her head slowly, in blatant disbelief. "No. There's no way he actually believed that. Surely not..."

I shrug, trying to appear nonchalant, like it doesn't still hurt after so many years. "He did. And he convinced my mother of it, too. They both hated me after that."

"How old was your sister?" Nora whispers.

"Four," I answer.

"And you?"

"I was six."

She stares back at me, her blue eyes unyielding. "You were six years old. Even if you had heard her, and I'm sure that you didn't, how could you have saved her? You were too little."

I meet her gaze without flinching. "Nora, I guarantee you. If I'd heard her get out of bed and walk outside, I would've saved her."

Nora smiles a sad smile. "I have no doubt that you would've."

We stand there for the longest time, and the air is heavy around us with the weight of our conversation.

"I can't believe I just told you all of that," I admit finally. "I've never told anyone before."

She glances up at me, her eyes soft.

"Not even Gabe?"

I shake my head. "No. Gabe and Jacey were only here in the summers. They never saw my sister, so they don't even know she existed. They saw the bruises my father gave me when I was a kid, but they never knew why."

"Didn't anyone ever try and take you away from your parents?" Nora asks softly, her eyes assessing me, raking me over, searching out my secrets.

I shake my head. "I never told anyone. Gabe knew, to some extent, but I made him swear not to tell. I guess kids are just always loyal to their parents, no matter what. But he and Jacey did their best to help me. They kept me down at their grandparents pretty much all summer, every summer."

But the winters were endless.

"Why does he want you to ring the bell?" Nora asks, her voice filled with dread.

I stare out the window. "Because that used to be his thing. He thought I purposely didn't save my sister because I was scared to swim. So he'd come home from the bar and drag me out to the beach, where he'd try and make me swim out and ring the bell. It infuriated him when I wouldn't. He'd beat me senseless and I still wouldn't do it."

Nora sucks in her breath as she stares at me in sympathy.

"Don't feel sorry for me," I tell her firmly. "Because what he doesn't know is that I stopped being afraid of the water by the time I was ten. But I kept refusing out of principle...and stubbornness. I decided that he could beat me, but he couldn't make me pay for something I didn't do. It was my own way of standing up to him."

Nora's lips spread in a slow smile. "So that's why you *can* swim, but you *don't*."

I nod, curtly, one time.

"And now he's trying to bully you into swimming," she realizes. "One last time."

I nod again.

But Nora's confused again. "I don't get it though," she says. "You said your mom has hated you ever since. Why would your father think that using her as leverage would work?"

I look away from her. "Because one of the things he used to tell me was that I was weak. That I was too loyal, that I should be colder. Like him."

Nora stares at me, horrified. "He faulted you for being a good human being?"

I shrug. "I guess. He saw kindness as a weakness. And he always called me weak. I guess he wants me to either show, once and for all, that I *am* weak, or show that I can be a cold-hearted bastard like him."

Without another word, Nora throws herself into my arms with enough force to knock me backward. We tumble into the chair behind us and she lands on my lap.

"Is your leg ok?" she asks quickly.

I nod. "Yeah. Don't worry about it." My knee is throbbing, but I don't care. It doesn't matter.

She looks into my eyes. "You're not weak, Brand. Being kind is not a weakness. You're the farthest thing from weak that I've ever seen in my life."

I don't answer.

She lays her head on my chest, remaining still. After a while, she speaks without moving.

"I can hear your heart."

I don't say anything.

"You have the strongest heart of anyone I've ever known."

I still don't say anything, although that fucking lump forms in my throat again.

Before long, Nora raises her head.

"Don't compromise yourself for him," she tells me, her blue eyes staring into my own. "I don't know what his game is. But don't let him compromise you. Do what's best for *you*. Do what you're comfortable with. No more, no less."

She stares at me fiercely for a minute before she kisses me, hard, with passion.

I kiss her back, pulling her into me, my arms wrapped around her.

She gets it. She's the first person to ever really 'get' my situation and the fucked-upedness that was my father. But the sad part is, I know she only gets it through experience of her own.

Because her father is just as fucked up in his own way as my father was.

That only pisses me off more.

But now, instead of only being pissed at a dead man, I'm pissed at someone living, at a situation that I can actually change.

Nora's dad isn't going to hurt her again.

Chapter Fifteen

Nora

I put my earrings in, small diamond studs that shine in the lobes of my ears. With a sigh, I look at my reflection.

My hair is pulled into a sleek chignon, I'm wearing makeup, and I've got on an evening dress, small and black.

With a heavy sigh, I glance at the clock.

We should leave soon. I both dread it and want to get it over with.

I spray on some perfume and venture out of my room to find Brand.

What I find takes my breath away.

Brand is leaning against the windows, waiting for me, dressed in a perfectly fitted black tux.

My breath holds on my tongue as I stop dead in my tracks and shamelessly stare.

Sweet Mary. I thought that there was nothing sexier on the planet than Brand Killien. I was wrong. Brand Killien in a freaking tuxedo is unbelievable.

He's lean, he's strong, he's tanned, he's blond. His blue eyes meet mine, and he smiles.

"See something you like?"

Gah.

My knees literally feel weak as I cross the room and kiss him softly on the lips.

He smells like the woods. And man. And Heaven.

"Maybe," I answer with a grin. "Do you have plans tonight? Because I have this thing…"

He shrugs. "I could make myself available. I mean, I'm dressed for it and all."

Yes, he certainly is.

I look him over again, at the way his shirt and jacket snugly skim his muscle, the way his pants hug his slim hips. I feel the butterflies fluttering around in my belly again, the adrenaline rush, rush, rushing through my veins.

He's mine.

For tonight.

For the summer.

I glance down. "Where's your knee brace?"

Brand shakes his head. "It's there. Under my pants."

"What else you got under there?" I purr, my hand running over his broad chest. Brand neatly catches my hand and restrains it with his own.

"Calm down, Tiger. As much as you'd like to distract me, we've got to get this dinner over with."

I sigh and I feel my shoulders droop. "Fine. Raincheck, then."

Brand's lip twitches. "Shall we go?"

I nod. Brand takes a step and I stop in my tracks.

"Where are your crutches?"

"I'm not using them tonight, doctor. I've got the brace on. The doctor told me I could bear weight as tolerated. It'll be fine."

I stare at him.

He stares back.

"You're stubborn," I sigh. He grins.

He limps, but he walks to the car unassisted.

After we're strapped into my car, I turn to him.

"If my father is rude to you, we'll leave."

Brand rolls his eyes.

"No, we won't. We'll do whatever it is that you need to go to do. It doesn't matter to me if your dad is rude. Trust me, I can take it."

His voice soothes me. His presence soothes me. His smile soothes me. Everything about him is calming, like a tonic, and I nod.

"Okay."

The drive doesn't take long, of course, and while I wish we could linger in the car out in the driveway, we can't.

Brand looks at me. "Ready?"

No.

"Yeah."

My mother opens the door before we even reach it, pulling me into a hug. She looks beautiful, of course.

"Ma belle fille," she sings, kissing my cheeks. "I've missed you."

She pulls me into the house in a cloud of Chanel No. 5. She looks over my shoulder.

"And you," she beams at Brand. "Thank you for everything you did for Nora that terrible day." She glances at his leg. "I'm so sorry you were hurt. It's terrible. Can I get you anything?"

I nod. "A water would be nice."

And a valium.

Brand shakes his head. "No, thank you, Mrs. Greene."

"Call me Camille," my mother instructs.

She leads us into the formal dining room which is dripping with gardenias and roses and lit candles are everywhere. The long table easily seats twenty, although only two are currently at it now.

My father and my brother, Nate.

William is no where in sight, thank God.

My father barely spares us a glance, doesn't even stop speaking to my brother. But Nate's face lights up and he gets out of his chair, crossing the room to envelop me in a hug.

I introduce him to Brand, and they shake hands and everything seems fine.

But then my father intrudes.

"This was a family affair, Nora," he chastises me. "I didn't tell you to bring anyone."

My mother breaks in, laying an elegant hand on his arm. "Maxwell, don't be rude. After all that Brand did for us, you should be nice."

Yes, Maxwell, be nice.

If looks could kill, I'd be murdering my father right now. What's that called? Patricide? Yeah. That.

My father glares at my mother and she pretends to ignore it.

Brand takes it all in stride... my father's rudeness, my family's very obvious dysfunction.

"I'm sorry to intrude," he says smoothly, shaking my father's hand. "Nora wasn't sure how large this gathering was going to be and she asked me to accompany her. I can't say no to her."

Hell no, he can't. I remember our day by the lake and smile inside. He might be stubborn, but I am too.

My father sniffs. "Try harder."

Oh my God.

Before I can make a retort, he returns to his chair, motioning to Nate to join him. Nate flashes me an *I'm sorry, but what can you do?* look before joining him.

I personally want to chase Maxwell Greene down and punch him in the face. *That's what I can do.*

But I don't.

Instead, I turn to my mother. "Do we have a few minutes before dinner?"

She nods.

"Great," I smile, putting my hand on Brand's elbow. "I'm going to show Brand your gardens."

She smiles, grateful that I'm distracting our guest from my father's rudeness. Once again, I wonder why she puts up with him. Other than the fact that she's thousands of miles from her homeland, and my father controls all the money.

I lead Brand out the massive French doors and onto the veranda overlooking the beach.

"I'm sorry," I tell him when we're alone. "I had a feeling he'd be like that."

Brand shrugs. "Like I told you, it's fine. I don't care what your father thinks of me. I've been in battle, Nora. Words don't hurt."

I smile a little, and shake my head, thankful for his understanding even if it's not true. Words do hurt. My father doesn't deserve to breathe the same air as Brand, much less be graced by his presence.

I motion to the gardens below us, the lush greenery, the roses.

"My mother's hobby," I say by way of explanation. "We have a gardener who helps her, a dear man who has been with us for a very long time, but my mother tends the roses herself. It's her getaway, I suppose."

Her getaway from her reality of my father.

I shudder. I can't imagine being married to him.

Brand stares down at all of it. "It's beautiful. Like you."

He turns to me, his eyes meeting mine, his hand splayed on my back.

"I don't know what's going on with you and your father," he says quietly. "But you've got this. I'm here with you, and you're going to be fine."

He must've noticed my shaking hands. Great.

I smile, putting every ounce of courage into it, to trick Brand into thinking that I'm brave.

I'm brave.

I'm fucking brave.

"I'm good," I assure him. "I've got this."

He nods. "I know you do. And your mom is gesturing to us. Shall we?"

We make our way back inside, and sit at our places. I'm at my father's left, Nate is at his right. My mom is across the table by Brand.

I feel like we're separated by an ocean and I look at him helplessly.

He stares at me pointedly.

You've got this.

I take a breath.

I'm actually fine for the first twenty minutes of dinner. My mother is chatting across the table with Brand, my father focuses his attention on Nate, and I'm left pushing my food around my plate, but I'm perfectly happy with that. As long as he leaves me alone I'm happy with that.

Until William walks into the room.

I feel like the temperature drops twenty degrees when he enters, and a chill runs down my spine. I stop chewing, I stop breathing.

"I'm sorry I'm late, Camille," William apologizes without a smile.

Ice water pumps through my veins at the sight of his face.

It's strange. I've known him my entire life, and while he made me uneasy throughout my teen years, I never knew why. I never knew that I should fear him... until last year.

"It's fine," my mother answers, her distaste apparent. "You didn't get back to me, so I assumed that you weren't coming. Let me get you a place setting."

She rises gracefully, and William circles the table to me.

"I'll sit by Nora," he announces.

My skin crawls as he bends and kisses my cheek.

Don't touch me, you ugly Fucker.

I want to burn it off. I want to race out of the room, go straight to the kitchen, dig out some matches and set my face on fire....all to burn off his lip prints.

"Hello, my dear," he murmurs as he sits down next to me. "You're hard to get a hold of."

I'm numb, frozen to my seat and all I want to do is bolt from my chair. William rests his arm on the back of my seat, his fingers lightly touching my back. As if he owns me. As if he has the right.

Across the room, Brand watches me like a hawk, his gaze intense, his eyes frozen to mine.

Are you ok?

I take a breath.

Yes. I nod, barely moving.

He stares at me still, unconvinced, ready to come to my aid.

He's right. I'm not ok.

I'm not ok.

But I have to pretend like I am.

Appearances are everything.

I keep eating, ignoring my father and Nate and William. I keep eating, keep pretending that this isn't happening, that I'm not at the same table, breathing the same air as the man who raped me mere months ago.

The man who raped me and then my father either didn't believe me, or didn't care.

My ears roar.

"Nora?" my dad raises his eyebrow. I can tell from his tone that this wasn't the first time he said my name.

"Yes?"

My cheeks flush.

"William just asked you to go sailing with him tomorrow. He'd like to discuss the Chicago deal with you. Answer him, please."

I look up at William and find him watching me with aging eyes. The wrinkles around his mouth tighten as he waits for my answer.

My stomach rolls.

I'm gong to throw up.

I swallow hard.

"You are the expert about that deal," I say carefully. "I haven't officially even started yet. William, you should discuss it with my father at this point."

My father shoots daggers with his glare, but I ignore it and sip at my water.

I can do this.

Brand is still watching me, still waiting to come to my aid. But he can't. Because this is a family affair. There's nothing anyone can do.

"I'd rather discuss it with you," William says, taking a swig of Scotch. "You're more agreeable than your father. But if tomorrow doesn't work for you, we'll do it another time."

I glance into his eyes and his are icy, dangerous. He's pretending to be understanding now. It won't last. When I'm alone with him… when I'm alone with him… when I'm alone.

My breath catches and I can't take another one.

I'm frozen.

My mother comes to my aid.

"Nora, if you're finished, can you come to my room? I'm taking a trip to France in a month or so and I'd like for you to look at something."

Thankfully, I nod.

Yes.

Thank you, God.

William stands when I do, and he presses my hand as I leave, his thumb biting into the pad of my palm. Hard. A warning.

Don't try and run from me.

Gratefully, I trail after my mother down the hall and I feel William staring at me as I leave. I don't look back, instead, I numbly stop in the bathroom and scrub my hand where he touched it before I join my mother in her room.

Silently, I pray that Brand will be all right with the piranhas back in the dining room.

My mother brings several items from her closet and searches my face.

"Are you all right?"

I nod. "Of course, why wouldn't I be?" Because she doesn't know. Because I'll never tell her. It's too awful. Too humiliating. *No one can ever know.*

"Are you ever going to tell me what happened? I know something did."

I paste a smile on. "Everything is fine. William is just... William."

My mother nods, unconvinced.

"He's difficult," she agrees. "He always has been. He... er, he was slightly in love with me when I was dating your father, back when I first came from France."

I stare at her in shock.

"Slightly in love? How can someone be *slightly* in love?"

My mother smiles tightly. "He was in love with me. He made some unwanted advances. I put him off. I was still in love with your father, you see."

Her words are so telling. She was still in love with my father then, unlike now.

"If he ever harms you, you must tell me," she instructs softly. "Don't go to your father. Come to me."

Her eyes are steely and determined, an expression I've never seen in them before. I stare into them, mesmerized.

"And what would you do?" I ask softly, before I can help myself.

"I would do what any mother would," she says firmly. "I would take care of it."

Her words send chills through my heart, because her face tells me she means it. Which further steels my resolve to never tell her. I can't have her doing something crazy and getting into trouble because of me.

I shake my head, even though I desperately wish I could spill it all to her.

"No, it's fine," I assure her, every word a lie. "He hasn't hurt me."

Lies.

My mother walks to her closet and pulls out several new items of clothing. "I'll be going to France in a month or so, darling. Would you like to go? You can get away from here. A break."

She's hopeful as she waits. But the only thing I can think of is Brand. I've only got a couple of months with him. I can't waste them by going to France, as much as I'd love to get away from here. Permanently, actually.

I shake my head.

"Any other time and I would, maman," I tell her. "But I can't leave right now."

She studies my face. "I see," she says softly. "You can't leave Brand Killien. I don't blame you."

She lays her clothes on the bed and pulls me over to look at them.

"There's a lot to be said for strength and honor," she tells me firmly, turning me around to look into my face. She pushes back a tendril of hair. "Money isn't everything. In fact, as I've gotten older, I've realized... money isn't anything."

I shake my head and point to the pink outfit. "That one. And what are you talking about?"

She smiles, because she knows full well that I'm following her point.

"If you love someone, don't let money or lack of money, stand in your way. Being a good person is far more valuable."

It is. I know it is. And that's the reason that I can't truly be with Brand. He's far too good for me.

But I smile. "I know, maman. But why are you telling me these things? Your life has turned out okay, has it not?" I decide to go with the pretense that they've always kept, and that I've pretended to believe for the past decade.

She looks away, and for the first time, she doesn't smile and gush about my father. Instead, she simply says, "Things aren't always what they seem, my sweet."

Her voice, so sad, startles me. "Are you ok?" I ask quickly. She smiles.

"Of course. I will be." She glances at the clothing again. "So you think the pink over the coral?" She changes the subject and I let her.

Because things aren't always what they seem and she doesn't want to talk about it.

That's ok. She's got her secrets and her feelings and her sadness, and so do I.

So I certainly understand the need to pretend.

I smile. "The pink. It complements your eyes."

And that is how we behave, almost always. Forget the issues, focus on the mundane. It's how we've always survived.

Chapter Sixteen

Brand

Five minutes after Nora leaves with her mother, Maxwell approaches me.

"Come have a scotch," he instructs me. It's not a request.

I decide to humor him. What he has to say might be interesting.

I limp to the sidebar where he pours me a scotch. I down it in one gulp, thumping the glass onto the bar, and turning back toward my seat.

"Thanks for the drink."

He grabs my elbow. I pause and stare pointedly at his hand and then at his face.

He lets go.

He's an asshole, but he's not stupid.

"Leave my daughter alone," he says bluntly. "I know you're having fun playing house, but you're not what she needs. Just bow out gracefully."

I turn back, his words stiffening my spine.

"I'm not what she needs?"

Maxwell shakes his head. To my left, I see Nate and William from my periphery. They're trying to pretend they aren't listening, but I know they are.

"You don't have the first clue what she needs," her father tells me icily. "You can't possibly. You're from another world, Killien."

I almost laugh. "I was exactly what she needed last week when I pulled her from the wreckage of that café. You know, when you were standing outside not doing a thing to help."

His jaw clenches and I see a vein tick in his forehead.

"She's twenty-three years old. She doesn't know what she needs. You're clouding her vision. If you really cared for her, at all, then you'd leave her alone and let her focus on what's important."

Again, I almost laugh.

"She's twenty-three years old. She's old enough to know what she needs. Perhaps you're the one who should leave her alone and let her figure it out."

I start to walk to my chair again, but his next words stop me cold.

"*I own her*, Killien. And I'll never let you be with her. Know that right now."

His words are ice and I whirl back around, but Nate jumps from his chair and rushes to defuse the situation.

"I'm sorry, Brand. My father is overwhelmed with work right now — under a lot of stress. I'm sorry. Please... come sit with me and tell me about the Rangers. It must've been damn fascinating."

I stare into Maxwell Greene's face, at his emotionless eyes, at his fixed mouth. He's a man who doesn't care about anyone but himself. I instantly take back my earlier thoughts that taking care of yourself is the smart thing to do. I never want to be Maxwell Greene.

I walk past him without another word, following Nate back to the table. William gets up to join Maxwell at the bar, leaving Nate and I alone.

"What is going on with this family?" I ask bluntly. "Nothing matters but business?"

Nate smiles an empty smile. "So you've caught onto that, huh?"

Like Nora, Nate has his mother's blue eyes, but instead of red hair, his is blond, cut short. He's tall and slim, and unlike Nora, I sense an ambitious hunger in him. With Nora, it's like it's something that makes her tired. She's used to trying to please her father, but it's not something she enjoys.

Nate seems to not only accept it, but thrive on it.

I nod. "Yeah. It's pretty apparent."

Nate chuckles. "Well, it's been drilled into our heads since we were babies. Be a Greene. Do what it takes, and all that. The business has been passed down from generation to generation for several hundred years. Our family came over with Columbus, you know. We've got big shoes to fill."

I glance over at Maxwell and William. They're chatting quietly, in intense conversation. Probably discussing mergers and acquisitions and how to eat their competition for breakfast.

"What did your dad mean when he says that he owns Nora?" I ask suddenly. It was such a strange thing to say. Nate instantly looks uncomfortable.

"He shouldn't have said that. He only meant… there's a contract, we both have one. When we finished high school, we were given a contract to work at Greene Corp in exchange for our college tuition and trust funds. No big deal."

No big deal?

"You had to sign a contract for your birthright?" I can't even keep the shock out of my voice. I was right. Maxwell is just as fucked up as my father was, every bit as controlling.

Nate nods, nonplussed. "It was no big deal, particularly because we've known since we were kids that we would work for Greene Corp. It's what we were born to do."

I drop the subject because clearly Nate doesn't see how fucked up it is.

Instead, I tackle a new one. Nate is being forthcoming with information, so I might as well push my luck for more.

"What's the deal with William?"

Nate glances at me.

"What do you mean?"

I nod toward William and Maxwell. "He seems very…attached to Nora. And very…. I don't know."

Nate chuckles. "Yeah. He's intense. He's always been that way. And as far back as I remember, Nora's been his favorite. He never got married and had kids of his own."

Yeah. The way William had been looking at Nora wasn't fatherly. But I don't point that out. Nate seems fairly oblivious to it, although I don't know how.

"I thought Greene Corp was family own and run?" I ask suddenly. "How is it that William seems to have such an important job?"

Nate stares at me in surprise, although he doesn't get annoyed at my blunt prying.

"William *is* family," he answers slowly. "He owns half of the company because he's my uncle. My father's brother."

The world seems to stop turning as I stare back at him, shocked, repulsed.

Nora's *uncle?*

I feel the sudden urge to lunge from this chair, find Nora, scoop her up and carry her out of this fucked-up madhouse.

"Your uncle?"

My words are wooden, stilted, as I try to wrap my head around it.

Nora's afraid of her uncle. Her uncle is sending her threatening text messages. And the look I see in Nora's eyes... it makes me dread knowing what he did to her.

But I know.

I know.

Nate nods. "Yeah. Our uncle."

Nora and Camille choose this minute to walk back in, and Nora instantly finds me, searching me out. I smile at her.

Everything's fine, don't worry.

She nods, just barely, her shoulders sagging a bit with relief.

She's in a house of sharks and she's worried about me.

She walks straight past everyone else and puts her hand on my shoulder. "I'm exhausted," she tells me. "Are you ready to go?"

I instantly push away from the table.

"Of course."

I thank Camille, and we walk out.

The entire time, I can feel the glares of William and Maxwell between my shoulder blades.

The entire time, my head is spinning.

Her uncle.

Her fucking uncle.

As we turn the corner, I glance back into the dining room, and see William watching Nora leave. His gaze is rapt and he's focused only on her.

My stomach rolls.

"I forgot something," I tell Nora. "Go ahead. I'll be right out."

She looks up at me, confused, but I don't say another word. Instead, I just walk back into the dining room, trying very very hard not to limp.

I walk straight up to the bar where William is refilling his glass.

He glances at me in surprise, and I lean in to speak in his ear, where only he will hear me.

"If you put another fucking hand on Nora, I'll crush all of your fingers, then break them off and feed them to you. Got it?"

William's head snaps back and he stares at me, his eyes wide and filled with guilt.

"I don't know what she's said to you," he snaps quickly. "But she's lying."

I shake my head slowly, and look into his faded eyes.

"She didn't tell me anything. You just did."

His hand is clutching the edge of the bar, so I make a fist and lean on his hand, crushing it under my weight. No one else in the room can see it but the two of us.

"As I said," I growl softly. "Touch her again, and you won't have hands left to touch anyone else. And that will be the least of your worries."

I take my fist away from his hand and he glares at me.

"You don't have the slightest idea what you've just done," he snaps. "I have the power to be your worst enemy."

I smile slowly.

"Bring it."

I walk out of the dining room, careful not to limp. The last thing I see before I turn the corner is the satisfied expression in Camille's eyes.

Nora is waiting for me by her car, out where the air smells like the lake and the night breeze ruffles her hair. Her eyes are big in the dark.

"What did you forget?"

I shrug.

I forgot to threaten your uncle.

"It's not important. You ready to go home?"

Home.

Where we live together.

For now.

Her eyes widen at the word and she nods immediately and without question.

"Yeah."

She drives and the night blurs past us outside the window. I don't mention her uncle and neither does she.

The quiet is all encompassing, but it isn't uncomfortable.

Finally, I look at her.

"You ok?"

She smiles, a small tiny movement.

"Yeah. You?"

"Of course."

She smiles wider and pulls into the drive. "Let me go in and get your crutches. You've been without them all night. I know your knee must be killing you."

I shake my head. "It's fine. I can walk."

I limp, but I walk unassisted into the house. *I'm no pussy, goddamnit.* Although I can't deny that pain streaks from my knee down to my ankle.

Fuck it.

As soon as Nora walks through the door, she starts shedding clothing. First her shoes, then her dress, then her bra, then finally her panties. When she stands in front of me stark naked, she smiles, her first real smile of the night.

"Ready for bed?"

I smile.

"Always."

We tumble into bed together and Nora presses her body into mine, limp against me, warm and soft. She runs her fingers down my chest, over my hips, and cups my balls.

I close my fingers over her hand.

"Not tonight, sweetheart."

Because you need to know that you're more than a fuck.

I hear her sudden intake of breath. "What?"

"Not tonight. I just want to lie here with you. Does that work for you?"

I pull her even closer, until her hips are pressed to mine and our legs are twined together.

"I guess," she grumbles, "But I was hoping for a little more of this."

She strokes my dick.

The traitorous bastard springs to life, but I ignore it.

Cold Fish. Cold Fish. Cold Fish.

"Not tonight," I remind her. "We don't always need to do that, you know."

Because she's more than just that. Whatever happened to her... I have the feeling it skewed her perception of herself.

Her eyes narrow in the night.

"I know we don't have to," she says finally. "I just like to. With you."

After that clarification, she puts her head on my chest and is silent for a few minutes, until finally, her voice is small in the night.

"Thank you for going with me tonight."

"You're welcome."

I wrap my arms around her and hold her until we fall asleep.

Chapter Seventeen

Nora

He doesn't want me.

I gulp hard, trying not to move because Brand thinks I'm sleeping.

I shouldn't have taken him to dinner tonight because now he knows what I am. I don't know how, but he knows. I saw it in his eyes earlier, and now he doesn't want me.

I hold a fist to my mouth to keep the sounds from slipping out.

I want to go outside and scream to the moon, but I can't.

I'm tainted.

I'm used.

I'm unworthy.

He knows.

He knows.

He knows.

Without meaning to, I whimper. Brand stirs in his sleep, his heavy arm strewn across my waist.

I've got to get out of here. The walls are closing in. I've got to move.

I quietly try to slip from bed, but Brand's arm tightens, pulling me even more closely to him. Even if he knows, he's still here. He still wants to share this bed with me. He still wants to touch me.

So I'm even more curious now. What *exactly* does he know?

I wait, inhaling and exhaling deeply, calmly. After a few minutes more, I try to move again. This time, I'm able to slip away.

When I reach the door, I grab Brand's shirt and put it on in lieu of a robe. The sleeves fall way past my hands, so I shove them up as I grab a bottle of wine and uncork it in the kitchen.

I don't bother with a glass. I simply take the bottle and start to walk outside, when my phone buzzes on the counter.

Dread fills me, instantly and completely.

Which will it be? My father or my uncle?

I force myself to look, only to find William's name.

You fucked up. So did your boyfriend.

Startled, I stare at the words. *So did your boyfriend.* What did Brand do?

I grab my phone and the bottle of wine, and head outside for some air. I walk down to the beach, dropping into the sand, not worried about the fact that I don't have underwear on and sand will get into all of my business.

It doesn't matter.

Nothing matters.

The words on my phone threaten to burn my hand, so I drop the wretched phone and take a swig of wine. Directly from the bottle. My mother would be so proud.

I take another.

Then another.

Then, when the liquid courage has begun circling through my veins, I pick the phone back up.

What do you mean?

I don't even have time to put the phone back down before there's an answer.

You should've known not to fuck with me.

Chills run down my spine. I didn't fuck with him. I *do* know better.

I can't breathe.

He's threatening Brand.

I stare at the words again and they run together and I can't breathe.

So instead, I drink because I don't know what else to do. I won't know what he intends to do until William actually does it, so all I can do is wait.

Wait for the other shoe to fall.

I sit in Brand's shirt in the sand, smelling his scent on my skin and drinking wine as I stare at the stars.

Before long, after most of the bottle is gone, my nose goes numb and my fingertips get cold.

I take the last drink left in the bottle, then cast it aside.

I don't know when I fall asleep.

All I know is that the sand feels ever so good against my cheek.

Chapter Eighteen

Brand

I wake up in the middle of the night alone, although it doesn't take long to find Nora.

She'd left the front door wide open. Her car is still in the drive, so I wander down to the beach.

That's where I find her passed out in the sand. She's wearing my tuxedo shirt, and an empty bottle of wine is about a foot away from her, resting in the dirt.

She's had a hard night.

Obviously.

I ignore the twinges in my leg and bend, scooping her up and carrying her back into the house. Each step is torturous with the added weight on my knee, but there's no way I'm leaving her outside.

She nestled into my chest without waking, and I find that one side of her face is covered in sand. As are her arms and legs.

With a sigh, I carry her into the bathroom. I bend and lay her in the tub, and remove the hand-held sprayer before I turn the water on. I let it get warm in the sink, before I pick it back up and rinse off her legs, her feet, her arms.

She doesn't stir until I'm wiping her face off with a washcloth.

She wakes with a start, her hands automatically flying up to shield her face.

"No!" she protests wildly, her eyes glazed, striking out at me, clenching her hands into fists, blows raining onto my chest.

"It's just me," I grab her hands, restraining her. "Shhh. It's ok. It's only me."

She flails for just a moment longer before her eyes register who I am and she breathes my name. "Brand."

She doesn't question why she's naked in the bathtub or why I'm bathing her. She doesn't say anything, actually. She just lets me wash the dirt away.

When I'm finished, I ask her to stand up and she does it obediently.

I towel her off. She's so drunk, she's only hovering on the edge of consciousness. I know that the second she's in bed, she'll pass out once again.

Her eyes are still closed as she stands.

But then, as I pull the towel away, she opens them.

"Why don't you want me, Brand?"

I yank my hands away from her in surprise.

"What?"

Her eyes are bleary, her voice soft and slurred.

"You don't want me anymore. Although I don't know that you ever really did." She raises her arms and I help her out of the tub. She wobbles, then clings to me to steady herself.

"Is it because I'm so used?"

My gut clenches at the vulnerable sound of her voice, at her words, at the soft and sad expression in her eyes. Even though she's drunk, maybe especially because she's drunk, she's a wide-open book.

"You're not used," I tell her firmly, as I pick her up back up in my arms. My knee protests, but I ignore it as I limp down the hall to the bedroom. "You're not used."

She rests her head against me, her arms slung around my neck.

"I am," she whispers. "But I never wanted to be."

I don't bother putting a nightgown on her, instead, I carry her to bed naked. I nestle her into the sheets and sit on the side of the bed, resting my throbbing knee.

I thought she was going to pass out right away, but she opens her eyes again.

"Will you stay with me?"

I nod. "I'll be right here."

Her eyes flutter closed, her lashes a black fringe against her pale cheeks.

She's so vulnerable, so soft and fragile. I can't imagine anyone hurting her. I can't imagine anyone rejecting her for things that happened out of her control.

"I do want you," I whisper to her, my hand on hers. "I do."

But she's sleeping now, passed out and oblivious to the world's ugliness and troubles. Her breathing is light and steady.

But I know there's no way I'm going back to sleep.

Instead, I grab my laptop and I sit in the chair by the window. I promised her I would stay and so I will.

I punch the name into the search engine and read the multitude of articles that are returned.

William Shepard Greene II.

The oldest son of William Shepard Greene I, older brother of Maxwell. Heir to half of the Greene fortune when their father passed. He's lauded highly in the business world, known for his keen instinct and sharp dealings.

He's older than Maxwell by ten years. He's sixty-two.

The mere idea of his hands on Nora turn my stomach and I glance at her again. She sleeps softly, curled onto her side, her hands by her face. She sighs in her sleep and my gut tightens again.

How dare he put his hands on her?

Why didn't anyone stop it?

I already know the answer. Because business comes first in the Greene household. I saw that firsthand tonight. And Camille... she doesn't give a fuck about the business, but she feels powerless to stop anything in that house. I can see that, too. Maxwell is the powerhouse in that family, and everyone else are his pawns.

Fucking rich people.

Rolling my eyes, I put the laptop away and crawl back into bed, careful not to disturb Nora. I pull her into my arms though, and keep her sprawled comfortably on my chest.

Here in the night, in this bedroom, there's no one but her and me.

That's how I want it to stay, although that very notion scares the shit out of me.

I can't put myself out there again. I've been through the bloody hills of Afghanistan, but there's nothing scarier than opening yourself up to someone else, only to get shattered.

I've been through that before, and I don't want to do it again.

With a groan, I run my hands over Nora's perfect bare ass.

Everything in me reacts, my heart pounds, my dick twitches, my groin contracts.

Somehow, I'm guessing I won't have a choice.

I'll end up laying myself out there.

I only hope there's pieces of me left when it's all over.

***

I wake in the morning to someone staring at me.

I open my eyes to find Nora on her elbow, her hair tickling my mouth.

"Good morning," she says softly. Her mouth is full and lush, and suddenly, I want to kiss it.

So I do.

She kisses me back, soft, then firmer, before she pulls away.

"I…uh. I thought I was on the beach last night," she murmurs, looking away and staring out the window. Her cheeks are flushed.

I nod. "Yeah. You were. But I brought you in, cleaned you up and put you to bed. The next time you want to finish off a bottle, can you just do it in on the couch?"

I'm joking, but she blushes even more, the flush spreading to her chest.

"I'm sorry," she tells me. "I don't know what came over me. I'm sorry."

"Don't be sorry," I answer quickly. "It's fine. You had a hard night."

She rolls on top of me, her hands on either side of my face, her legs straddling my hips.

"I don't remember, so if I said anything embarrassing, please just forget it," she pleads prettily, her hair falling into my face in a cascade. "I'll make it worth your while."

She wiggles her hips, grinding into my groin, which of course reacts. My dick springs to life, pressing into her and she smiles in satisfaction.

"Maybe you do want me," she says huskily.

"I do," I agree, remembering her pitiful question from last night. *Why don't you want me?*

As I stare into her beautiful face and I see all the questions in her eyes, the insecurities, the doubts, I do the only thing I can do… the only thing I think will help.

I show her how much I want her.

You're not used.

My hips flex.

You're beautiful.

I run my hands over her back, her shoulders, her hips.

Inside and out.

I push my fingers into her, sliding them out, then back in. Her neck arches, she sighs.

I can't say the things I'm thinking, because she doesn't want to talk about it. Because she thinks that I don't know. Because talking about it with me would kill her.

So instead, I show her what I'm thinking.

You're worthy.

You're beautiful.

You're mine.

I plunge inside of her, deep inside, claiming her for my own, for now, for the summer, for as long as she'll let me.

You're mine.

I press my forehead to hers as we rock together, as I claim her over and over and over.

You're mine.

She's trembling when we're done, limp in my arms as I hold her.

Mine.

Chapter Nineteen

Brand

Days are seamless here now.

We chat on the porch, we sit on the pier, we lie together in the hammock at night, watching the stars.

Each day, I think Nora will confide in me.

Each day, I think she'll trust me enough to tell me what William did to her. I know, in my gut, what it was. But I can't know it for a fact until she tells me.

Each day, she doesn't.

Each night, I hold her until she falls asleep.

Each night, I try and steel myself against her, to keep from getting sucked in further.

Each day, I try not to trust the feelings that are growing, the attachment, the tenderness, the bond.

Each day, I realize I'm failing.

***

Nora

I watch Brand sleeping on the couch with a book on his chest. He'd fallen asleep an hour ago and ever since, I've watched him.

He's so peaceful when he sleeps, his face so open.

I could watch him all day and all night.

But my phone dings, distracting me, filling my heart with dread.

I know… I know… the other shoe is getting ready to drop.

These past days have been too good, too comfortable, too perfect.

I approach my phone, and as innocuous as it seems lying on the kitchen counter, it might as well be poison, because when I pick it up and read William's words, the toxin runs through my veins, pulsing through my heart.

I want to see you. Sunday. In the conference room of Greene Corp, just you and me. 2pm. Be there. You don't want to know what will happen if you don't show up. But here's a hint: It involves your boyfriend.

I knew he'd been threatening Brand the other night with his text. *You and your boyfriend fucked up.*

I knew it. And I've been waiting with bated breath, every day, to see what he was going to do.

And here it is.

I've been summoned.

I'll finally know.

I glance at Brand and I literally have to fight the urge not to shudder over what I've done. Being here could've put him at risk. Every day I wanted to tell him, every day I didn't .

Each day, he's been nicer and nicer to me, making it impossible for me to want to ruin it.

I didn't want this fake little bubble that we've built here to burst… even though it was never real in the first place.

I should've told Brand from the very beginning that I'm encased in a bubble, my bubble is made of Swarovski crystal, and at the whim of my uncle or my father, I would drop to the floor and shatter.

But I didn't.

Because I'm too selfish.
But the clock was ticking… seconds, hours, days.
And the time has come.
The other shoe is going to drop.

Chapter Twenty

Nora

I can't let him go.

I watch him as he sits on the beach, staring at the fucking buoy that taunts him.

I know I should. I know I should cut the strings right now and walk away, but I'm not strong enough. I need him.

I need him.

Something has changed in him, something important, but I don't know what. His expressions soften whenever he looks at me and I can feel the change when he holds me at night. He's tender and his touch is ever so soft, a glaring contrast to the hardness of his body.

He's a trained killer, an Army Ranger. He's capable of so many dangerous things, but when he's with me, his touch is feather light. Careful.

Like I might break, like he suspects that I'm made from crystal, like he wants to protect me from shattering.

Warmth gushes through me at the thought.

Somehow, he's opened himself to me. He wants me. And as much as I thought I couldn't expose him to me, because I might taint him, and somehow take his goodness away, he's still Brand.

He sleeps with me every night, and he's still as good as he ever was.

Is it possible that I could be with him and not tarnish him?

Am I delusional to even hope?

There would be complications, of course, but there always is in life. He sees me for who I am. And he doesn't ask questions. He just sees me.

My heart wants to burst from the mere happiness of it all.

So much so that I want to do something for him.

Right now.

Before the other shoe drops and my world crashes down.

While I'm still strong.

Before I break on the floor in front of him into a million pieces.

I get up and march outside, straight to where Brand sits.

"Call that lawyer," I tell him. "We're taking care of this today."

Brand stares up at me in surprise, his long legs stretched out in front of him.

"What do you mean? Take care of what?"

I put my hands on my hips.

"I know I told you to handle your father's will however you want to handle it. And I meant that. But I know you, Brand. You don't back down from anything. Ever. Ring the bell, Brand. And don't ring it for him... ring it for you. Ring it so that you can put all of that ugliness behind you--- so that from now on, whenever you see a lake or an ocean or a buoy... you won't think of ugliness. I'm going to swim with you. We're going to do it together. Because I'm with you, Brand. I'm with you."

He stares up at me, dumbfounded and then he simply nods.

"Okay."

I raise an eyebrow. "Okay?"

He nods. "Yeah. Let's do it."

He pulls out his phone, punches in a number and waits.

"Todd? Come out to the beach. I'm taking a swim this morning."

He slips the phone back into his pocket and gets up.

"Should you wear a bathing suit, or are you planning on making Todd's day?"

I roll my eyes and laugh and we stroll to the house to change.

"You don't have to give everything to your mom, you know," I tell him. "You can do whatever you want with it. You need to take this swim for you, Brand. Not for her, not for him and not for me. You need this… to be free from them."

He stops, turns and pulls my face to his, kissing me as thoroughly as I've ever been kissed.

He pulls away and doesn't say a word. He doesn't have to. Everything he had to say was in that kiss.

We change and head back down to the beach. Todd arrives a few minutes later, holding a paper in his hand.

"It has to be from the beach behind your parents' house," he announces without preamble. "That's part of the stipulation."

"Fine," Brand tells him, and without another words, stalks down the beach. He's barely even limping.

I follow behind, and before long, we're standing behind Brand's childhood home. The buoy looms huge and haunting out in the lake, tilting with the waves. I shudder when I think that his sister died out here…. and that his father used to beat him right where I'm standing.

I feel someone staring at me, and as I look over my shoulder, I see Bethany Killien standing at her windows, watching us. Her face is set, and firm, and I don't see any softness there. I shiver, and turn back around.

Today isn't about her.

I grab Brand's hand.

"Let's do this."

He nods.

And then he walks straight into the water, as if he'd never ever been scared of it. He dives under the surface with purpose and for a moment, I forget that I'm supposed to be swimming with him. All I can do is watch the strength with which he glides through the water, his strong arms pulling him through, stroke after stroke.

I'm mesmerized for a moment, until I remember that I'm supposed to be with him, so I follow his lead and dive into the surf.

***

Brand

The water is frigid, of course. Because it always is. It doesn't matter if it's August or November, Lake Michigan always feels like ice water.

But I don't flinch or hesitate. I plunge in, and swim toward that motherfucking buoy.

Each time I surface, I take a breath and dive back in.

The water is clear, and cold, and everything I detest. But with each stroke, I realize that it isn't the water I detest. It isn't the lake. It isn't even that fucking buoy.

It's my father.

With every stroke, I shove his memory further away, decimating his power over me.

He doesn't control me anymore. I'm not the kid that I used to be.

Nora's right.

He'll never control me again.

With strong, even strokes, I approach the buoy, gulp for air, and then explode through the surface, grabbing onto it. I cling to the buoy for a second, before I violently shake it, to and fro.

The bell rings out clearly, into the air, all the way to the beach. I glance toward my parents' house and see the curtains of the living room fold close. My mother had been standing there, but she walked away.

That's fine. I'd expect nothing less.

I ring the bell again, then again.

The sound is eerie and haunting and if I concentrate hard enough, I can almost envision my little sister standing on the beach, waving at me.

I smile at the thought, at the memory of Allison. Through all of my father's beatings, at least he could never take that away. I loved my sister, and she loved me, and it wasn't my fault that she died.

Ring the bell, Brand.

I ring it one more time, hard and fast.

Consider it rung, asshole.

Nora reaches me now and flings herself at me, and we both cling to the buoy. She's wet and excited and wraps her arms around my neck, kissing me hard.

"You did it!" she cries out. "You did it."

I know there was never a question. I was going to do it. *I'm no pussy.*

But I kiss her back and don't say a word.

"Let's go back to shore," I finally tell her when we break for air. "I hate this fucking buoy."

She laughs and we swim for shore. I chase her and grab her foot, she laughs and twists in the water. It's as if I'm free now. Free from the constraining hate, free from the bitterness, free from all of it.

But then we reach the shore and reality awaits.

Todd waits.

My mother waits.

She's come out of the house now and stands disapprovingly on the shore with the attorney, watching Nora and I frolic in the water.

"I'm glad you're taking this so seriously," she says icily, looking down her nose at us.

Nora's head snaps back and before I can stop her, she stalks over to my mother and stares down at her.

"You have no right," Nora snaps, each word a pellet of ice. "You have no right to even be here. You have no right to hate Brand. You have no right to him at all. *You don't have the right.* You forfeited any rights to him years ago. If he gives you anything at all, it will be a miracle, because you don't deserve it."

I grab her elbow and pull her away. "Come on," I tell her firmly. "She's not worth it."

"Does your girlfriend know that you killed your sister?" my mother calls from behind us. The words stab me in the back and I stop, frozen in place, before I turn.

"She knows everything."

With that, I start to walk away again, but my mother just can't help herself. She has to keep prodding.

"Everything?"

The meaning of that one word is clear. Crystal fucking clear.

Everything. By *everything*, she of course means that my entire life is a lie. Everything I am, everything I've become... is a lie. In her eyes, anyway. Because she believes me to be a monster.

I'm frozen.

Completely still.

And Bethany Killian is as foreign to me as a stranger. She laughs.

"I didn't think so."

She spins on her heel and starts to walk back into the house, and anger wells up in me, red and hot, a fury that I haven't felt in years. It's so fierce that it clouds my vision, it's everything I have bottled up inside of me....all the anger that I've been carrying with me for so many years.

It explodes within me like a volcano.

"Mom?" The word is as foreign to me as she is.

She stops, and turns halfway around. She doesn't answer, but she looks at me.

"Go pack a bag. You have five minutes."

Now she speaks. "What?"

"You heard me. Go pack a bag."

She takes a step. "I don't understand."

"You don't have to. Go. Pack. A. Bag. Take anything you want from the house. It will be the last time you're inside."

My mother looks at me uncertainly, and for the first time, I see a real emotion on her face. Fear.

She's afraid to believe that I'm serious.

"You're not kicking me out of my own house," she says hesitantly, her eyes searching mine. "You wouldn't."

I have to fight a sneer. "I wouldn't? Why wouldn't I? What exactly have you brought me in life except for pain? Tell me that. Tell me one good thing you've ever done for me, and I'll let you stay."

My mother stares at me, looks away at the lake, lifts her chin and stares back at me.

"I brought you into this world."

I shake my head. "Wrong answer. You brought me into the world, true. But I didn't ask for that. And once I was born, you didn't do a thing for me. It was bad before Allison died, but after that, it was unbearable. Not only did you allow my father to beat the shit out of me every time he came home drunk from the bar, but you tried to make a helpless kid believe that he killed his sister. You're the fucking monster, not me."

My mother's eyes turn icy and she glares at me. "You *did* kill your sister. You heard her, Brand. I know you heard her and you let her walk into the lake. You could've stopped her, but you didn't."

An eerie calmness descends upon me and for once, I don't feel rage as I look upon my mother.

"I was six years old. I was upstairs asleep. I realize that when bad things happen, people blame someone when they're grieving. It's human nature. But to focus your grief and your rage on a six-year old kid... that was unforgivable."

My mother's eyes water and she looks away.

"My daughter died, Brand. You could've saved her... if only you'd listened for her. You were supposed to watch out for her. She was your little sister."

Her voice dwindles off and she wipes at her eyes. Nothing in me softens at her show of sadness.

"I was six years old," I reply. "*You* were supposed to watch out for her. Dad forgot to lock the door, not me. All of these years, if you had to have someone to blame, you should've blamed him. If you really are too small of a person to realize that sometimes accidents happen. Bad things happen. And sometimes there's simply no one to blame. You're a small, small person."

"My daughter died," she whimpers.

"Your daughter *did* die," I tell her coldly. "But you didn't have to lose both your children that night. That was a decision that you made. You're paying for that decision now. Go inside and get your things."

She looks up in disbelief and I see it in her eyes... she thought her show of tears would sway me. She was only trying to pull my strings... once again. Just like when I was a kid and she tried to make me believe I was a monster, that I'd killed my sister, that my father was only doing what he 'had to do' when he was beating me.

My blood chills as I look at her and all I can feel is distaste. For my own mother. Even worse, I see the exact same emotion in her eyes as she stares back at me.

She hates me and it is apparent.

"Go." I repeat. My voice is like ice.

She spins around and stalks away. I watch her disappear into the house, I watch the old peeling door slam behind her, I watch how the windows of the house seem to mock me, like large eyes that watched my father beat me on the beach, time and time again. This house is a tomb of bad memories. And I don't think I can look at it any longer. In fact, I don't even want it to exist.

I want all of it to just go away.

I turn to Nora.

"Could you do me a huge favor? Could you run down to the cottage and get the gas can from the garage and a box of matches?"

Nora stares at me, paralyzed.

"Please?" I prod.

She nods, confusion in her eyes, but she doesn't question me. She just takes off running down the beach barefoot. I watch her for a minute, then turn to the attorney.

"The house is mine now, correct?"

Todd nods. "Yes. Everything in it. And the woodshop and the garage in town. And the assets from the business. Everything."

"Good."

Todd eyes me uncomfortably. "What are you planning?"

I level a gaze at him. "A bonfire."

He stares back in apprehension. "That's arson."

"Not if I don't make an insurance claim," I tell him. "I simply want to get rid of the house so that I can clear this land and start fresh. I might even build another house here in the future. So that's not arson. That's demolition."

"You need a permit for demolition, son."

I narrow my eyes. "I'm not your son. And if Angel Bay PD wants to fine me, so be it."

Todd continues to stare at me uncertainly. "Okay. Well, this is yours now, too."

He hands me the key to the wooden box my father left for me and I shove it in the pocket of my swim trunks. I'll deal with that later.

Nora returns just as my mother walks down the steps with a suitcase in her hand. She jogs up to me with the gas can and matches, and my mother's eyes widen, the first real reaction I've seen from her.

I walk up to her.

"Mom, I loved you for the longest time, long after you stopped deserving it. I don't hate you now. I don't. But I'm done with everything toxic in my life, and that includes you. I'm going to sign over dad's business to you. I'm going to give you the money he had in the bank, his truck, his workshop. But I'm not giving you this house. I'm getting rid of every bad memory I have of this place today."

She sputters and then stops as she sees the expression on my face.

"You're serious."

"Dead serious."

Without another word, I shake gasoline out of the can all over the porch and fling it up on the walls.

I look at my mother.

"You might want to get back."

She takes a step back, then another.

I pause. "I know that I'll probably never see you again after you leave here today. And I'm okay with that. I can't deal with the all the toxins of my childhood anymore. If you ever want to have a real relationship with me, the normal kind of mother-son relationship, then look me up. Until then, take care of yourself."

I turn away and my mother hurries to her car without a word. She drives away without looking back and I have no doubt that I'll never see her again.

It does hurt, but I swallow it, because I know I have to let it go. If I'm ever going to get past everything that happened here, I have to let it all go.

I toss a match onto the house.

It ignites immediately and the heat presses against us, trying to push us away from it, almost like it's trying to protect itself from destruction.

It doesn't work, because I toss another match, then another.

It burns quickly.

I watch the flames lick at the sky, the smoke spiraling into the heavens. Every bad memory I have spirals away with it. One after the other, after the other.

It's surprisingly cleansing and with every board that burns, I feel weights being lifted from my shoulders.

I'm not guilty of anything. And I'll never have to look at anything or anyone again who tries to pretend otherwise.

Nora comes up from behind and wraps her arms around my waist as we watch it burn. Her cool arms bring comfort, the kind of comfort that only comes from someone who accepts me for who I am.

"You ok?"

I nod. "Yeah. You?"

"Yeah."

We watch the flames for a while, the oranges and blues and reds, before we walk away, down the beach to the only house that ever truly felt like home to me.

Chapter Twenty-One

Nora

I can't believe that just happened.

Brand literally burned his past down.

It's astounding. Overwhelming. Exhilarating.

And it's nothing short of what I would expect from him. He's so decisive. When he takes control of something, he doesn't do it halfway. The mere thought sets my belly aflutter.

I hear the shower running as Brand washes away the lake water, the ash from the fire and probably some bad memories, too. I know how that goes. I curl up on the sofa and give him his privacy. He deserves some solitude after what he just did.

As I lay still, I can't help but stare at the little wooden box.

It's fascinating to me. Ebony wood with an ivory inlay. Black and white. I have to wonder if his father did that on purpose.... Did he contrast black with white as an analogy for life? Life isn't black and white.

Unable to stop myself, I pick it up, turning it over and over. I shake it lightly.

There's a solid clunking noise inside. Something in the box has some heft. With a man as hateful as Joe Killien apparently was, it's hard telling what he put in the box.

I get goose bumps as I remember horror movies of the past... when body parts and worse have been sent as messages. Quickly, I set the box down.

Surely Joe didn't put a body part in the box, but I'm not sure that I want to know what actually is in there.

"I'm curious too," Brand says from the hallway. I turn to find him standing there, a towel slung around his waist. I'd been studying the box so intently, I hadn't even heard the shower water turn off.

He takes a few steps into the room, his strong calves flexing with his movement. Each movement he makes is so lithe and controlled. He picks up the box and turns it over in his large hands.

"I want to know, but yet I don't want to give him that satisfaction," he finally says, turning to me. "Does that make any sense? I know he's gone and he'll never know if I look or not. But *I'll* know."

"So you're not ever going to look?" I ask quietly, in a tiny bit of disbelief. Because I know I'd never have that kind of willpower. I'd have to know. Even if what was inside killed me or fueled my guilt or hate. But this is just one more way that Brand and I are different. He's got willpower. I don't.

Brand shrugs and sets the box aside. "I don't know. Maybe I will. But see, it's taken me years to get to the place where I don't care what he thinks, or what he says. I think it's something inborn in every person.... you need the approval of your parents. For better or worse, you need to know that you've met their expectations, that you are good enough. I know that I never will. And that's something I've had to let go of—and get past. It's taken me a long time."

"But anyone would be proud of you," I begin to argue, but Brand holds up his hand.

"You don't have to do that. I know all the arguments. Jacey used to argue the same things. When I graduated West Point with honors, they didn't come. They didn't send a card. They didn't acknowledge it at all. I threw a party with Jacey and Gabe. When I made the Rangers, they didn't say anything, and again, I celebrated with

Jacey and Gabe. But at the same time, I didn't write home and tell them, either. It's been a two-sided road. I haven't held up my part, but neither did they."

I shake my head and interrupt because he can't stop me. "But they gave you very good reasons to stay away. Your father beat you. Your mother didn't stop it..."

Brand nods. "Yeah, I know. But life is fucked up. People get hurt, people are scarred, people are damaged and sometimes, things aren't meant to be fixed."

"And you're afraid if you looked in the box, it might mess up your resolution?"

He nods. "I guess. I just don't want to have to start back at square one and try to forgive them again."

I suck in a breath. "Have you forgiven them?"

He stares out the window. "I don't know. I try. But I guess, mostly, I just continually put it out of my mind so that I don't have to think about it."

"That's denial," I tell him needlessly.

He smiles grimly. "I know. But it works for me right now. So I'm not going to look in the box...not right now. I don't need to. There are other things I need to worry about. More important things."

I raise an eyebrow. "Such as?"

Brand grins. "Lunch. I'm starving."

I roll my eyes. "You're always starving."

"Lunch at the Hill?" he asks, his eyes twinkling. I nod.

"It's a date," he tells me and he disappears back down the hall to get dressed.

It's a date.

A date with Brand Killien.

Gah. Oh how the worm turns in life, from one moment to the next. You never know what's going to happen.

I pull my hair back into a low ponytail and within twenty minutes, Brand and I are walking into The Hill.

Together.

I've got my arm looped through his and Maria looks up from the cash register, her face lighting up like fireworks when she sees Brand.

She rushes to him, kissing his cheeks and muttering Italian endearments. He smiles and hugs her and she shows us to a table by the window.

"You let me know if I can get you anything else," she tells him before she bustles away. "I'll get you a special dessert."

I look at Brand over the top of my menu. "She really likes you."

"She's very loyal. She doesn't forget it when someone has done something for her. All I did was move her daughter's stuff to college."

"And come and help her cut brush, and do a bunch of other stuff outside after her husband died," I add. He glances up at me, surprised. I shrug. "She told me last time. You did a lot for her."

"And so did Gabe and Maddy, and even Jacey," Brand says simply. "Maria's good people. So was Tony."

We fall silent as we decide what to eat, then hand our menus over after we order.

Brand stares out the window. "I always forget how much I do like this little town," he muses absently. "I always associate it with ugliness because of my parents, but I had good times here, too. I spent most of every summer down at the Vincents' place. Gabe and Jacey shared their grandparents with me. They were good people, too. Their gran has always been the mom I never had."

Something about that statement and the softness in his eyes at the mere mention twinges my heart.

"I'm glad you had that with them," I tell him honestly. "It sounds like they filled a void in your life."

And oh my god, how I wished I could have helped do that. I was here every summer too. Only I was four years younger and back then... well, that might as well have been an ocean of time.

Brand nods. "Yeah. Their gran taught me a lot. She was full of good advice. She still is, actually. She's in a nursing home in Chicago."

I take a sip of water. "What kind of advice? I'm afraid I grew up without much of that. My father is very focused on business and my mother... well, she's very focused on trying to put on the appearances that everything is fine in the Greene household. There wasn't much sage advice floating around."

Brand looks at me. "Well, Gran taught me everything I know about women."

This definitely catches my attention. "And what is that?"

He smiles. "There's too much to list. She never hesitated to share her opinion."

The affection on his face at her memory warms my heart. They say that if you watch a man with his mother, it's a good indication of his character. But I know that if I'd seen Brand with his 'gran', that I'd have known all I ever needed to know about him.

"Well, share a couple of things," I urge him. "Remember, I didn't get much advice. I can borrow yours."

He chuckles. "Well, I'm not sure how helpful it will be for you. She focused a lot on advice about women....on what I need to know."

I wait.

He sighs. "Okay. Well, she said that women don't always know what they want, but they almost always know what they don't want. Sometimes it takes them a while to narrow it down by elimination."

I ponder that, then nod. "Yeah. She's right about that one. What else?"

"One time, when we were about sixteen or so, Gabe and I were at the beach with her. Apparently, I was staring at some girl in a bikini, and Gran slapped me on the back of the head and told me that women weren't 'vaginas with legs'. I then got a lecture about how women are more than just sex. It was the most humiliating discussion of my life."

I giggle at the mere thought. "Did Gabe get the talk too?"

Brand nods. "Yeah. He wanted to die. There we were, right out on the beach in front of God and everyone, including hot chicks in bikinis, and his grandma was talking about sex."

I giggle again. "She sounds awesome."

"She is," Brand says firmly.

Our waitress refills our drinks and I look at Brand.

"Did she give you any other valuable advice, or was it all about women?"

He rolls his eyes. "Oh, for a teenage boy, trust me, it's always about the women."

I stare at him drolly. He smirks.

"I wish I'd paid more attention to the things she told me back then," he admits. "She was really a wise lady, and unfortunately, because I was a stupid kid, I didn't remember it all. But there was something she told me once, after some girl broke my heart, that has always stuck with me."

I wait.

He doesn't say anything.

"And that was?" I prod.

"Well, this chick had screwed me over in a big way. She was pretty messed up. And I'd come to the conclusion that women weren't worth it, that they were more trouble than they were worth."

"I can see where you might think that sometimes," I nod. "What did your Gran say?"

"She said... Branden, the best things in life are worth the greatest risk. Sometimes, before we fall, we fly."

I stare at him, at the smile that lingers on his lips, and I can't help but fall just a little bit in love with this big strong man that has held onto such a sentiment from his 'adopted gran'.

Knowing him now is so different from being wildly in love with him as a teen.

There's so much more to him than I'd ever have guessed before.

"That's beautiful," I tell him simply. "You're right. She was very wise."

Brand nods. "She never pulled any punches. She warned me away from her own granddaughter, too."

This freezes my hand on my glass.

"What?" I manage to ask.

Brand chuckles. "She was very perceptive. She knew, even before I did, that I was falling for Jacey a long time ago. And she pulled me aside and in her very direct way, she told me that Jacey wasn't ready for a guy like me. That maybe she never would be... because Jacey needed someone to tame her. I was offended at first, because I thought she was saying that I wasn't man enough to do it."

That's what it sounded like to me, too, and I have to wonder if Gran even knows him at all.

"Then what did she mean?" I ask curiously.

"She said that I had a soft spot for Jacey and that I'd never be able to give her the tough love that would fix her. She said I'm the type of guy who will come to your rescue when I'm needed, and it wouldn't be fair to me if I was with Jacey, because I'd always be coming to her rescue. She said I need someone more considerate than that, someone who has their act together."

I swallow hard. "I think your Gran really was wise. She nailed you to a T."

But I don't have my act together.

Brand shrugs. "I don't know about that. But she was right about Jacey. I came to her rescue a hundred times over the years. If I'd been 'with' her, it would've been a hundred more. So, Gran was right."

Our food arrives now and as I'm eating the steaming pasta, I can't help but consider that.

Brand really is the kind of guy to come to a girls' rescue. And Lord knows that my life is fucked up. If he were with me, *really* with me, he'd constantly feel like he needed to save me.

I'm no better than Jacey.

I'm conflicted... between the desperate need that I have to be with Brand, to soak him up... and to let him go so that he's not hurt by me, or by my life.

When Maria had told me about Jacey before, I'd felt so high and mighty, so judging. But yet, I know that I have to meet my uncle tomorrow, and he's going to threaten Brand and me, and still I want Brand.

Still I want Brand, no matter the cost.

So really, when it boils down to it, I'm as selfish as Jacey ever was.

Chapter Twenty-Two

Brand

Talking about Jacey makes me uncomfortable.

Not because I still love her, because I don't. Not in that way.

But because I can see that it puts Nora on edge. That's the last thing I want. She's been edgy ever since the dinner at her parents'. I don't want to add to that.

"Jacey's happily married now," I remind her as I finish up my lasagna. "And I don't want her anymore."

"I know," Nora answers. "And I'm sorry. It's not even my business. Who you want and who you don't want are your business, not mine."

I put my fork down and eye Nora carefully.

"Since when?"

The entire time we've been together at the cottage, her actions have been contrary to that statement.

She shrugs. "I just realized that I don't have the right to dictate anything to you. That's all."

I narrow my eyes. This is new. And strange.

"Weren't you the one saying that the bullet has already left the gun and that there's no going back now?"

Something soft flits through Nora's eyes before she covers it up.

"Yeah. I did. But I can be selfish sometimes. Anyway, what would you like to do this afternoon?"

She changes the subject clumsily and now I'm the one on edge.

What the fuck?

I shrug, attempting to appear nonchalant. "I don't care. Want to go swimming?"

It's an attempt to lighten the mood. But Nora rolls her eyes.

"Let's not push it."

I raise an eyebrow. "Why? When we first came to the cottage, you went skinny-dipping by yourself. Perhaps we should go together. It'd be a whole different experience, I can assure you."

Nora's face brightens, the clouds clear, and she's happy again.

"Sure," she agrees. "I'm sure it *will* be far different."

I pay the check and we head back to the cottage.

As we walk inside, Nora looks at me. "It's broad daylight, you know."

I raise an eyebrow. "Your point?"

She grins. "I don't have one. I was just making an observation." She slips off her shorts. Then her shirt. Then tosses her bra and underwear onto the couch.

She stops still and stares at me.

"I see you haven't undressed yet. Are you scared?"

I strip off my shirt. "Nah. Just distracted."

I drop my shorts and underwear at her feet.

"Let's do it."

I grab her hand and pull her out the door, determined to not become distracted by the way her nipples point to the sky. Not yet, anyway.

When we reach the water's edge, she stretches, lifting her hands to the clouds and arching her chest toward me.

I pretend not to see, although my dick definitely stands up and takes notice.

Without preamble, I scoop her up, plunge into the water, and drop her unceremoniously into it.

When she sputters back through the surface, she's shrieking.

"This wasn't what I had in mind when I wanted to skinny-dip with you!" she calls out, chasing me through the water. I swim hard, away from her.

Cat and Mouse.

She's fast though, and when I slow just a bit, she catches me. Lunging out of the water, she slams her hands on my shoulders, dunking me.

I rocket back out of the water and kiss her hard.

She startles, then clings to me, her tongue burying itself in my mouth. She wraps her legs around my waist and I feel her, the very centermost part of her, pressed to my stomach.

It makes me instantly rock hard.

With her wrapped around me, I float a few feet inland to where my feet touch.

And then I don't hold back.

I run my mouth along her neck, kissing it where it arches. I nip at her ear and when she arches backward, I suck her nipples, drawing them into my mouth and teasing them into sharp points.

She grips my back, her fingernails digging into my skin as the cold lake water chills every part of us.

But we're heating each other up.

Nora reaches down and strokes me under the water, teasing my rigid hard-on into steel. I could etch glass with it now and she knows it. She smirks as she dips her own head and licks my nipples.

Payback.

But I trump her when I slide my fingers between her legs and directly into her.

Despite the water, she's still dripping wet.

For me.

"Let's go inside, shall we?" I murmur against her neck. She nods.

"Yeah. Skinny-dipping is overrated."

She's flushed, almost panting, something that satisfies me.

I did that.

I pick her up, carrying her to shore.

"I can walk, you know," she tells me, laughter in her blue eyes.

"But you're too slow," I answer. "I'm a man on a mission."

She laughs and I carry her toward the house, both of us as naked as the day we were born.

And then I stop still.

Because there, sitting on the porch waiting for us, is Jacey.

She looks tired, but she's still here, in the flesh, watching Nora and I approach, in all our birthday suit glory.

Nora sucks in her breath.

"Is that…"

"Yeah. That's Jacey."

She squirms in my arms, but I hold tighter.

"You're more concealed if I carry you," I point out.

"But you're not," she answers. I shrug. There's no help for that now. We're both naked. But at least my arms wrapped around her will provide her with just a little bit of cover.

Jacey stands as we approach and there's laughter in her eyes. And confusion. I see her study Nora, trying to figure out who she is.

"Brand!" she calls out. "I see you're doing better… there was no need to worry after all!"

"Is that why you're here?" I answer. "Because you were worried? You could've called."

She grins and takes a step off the porch, her eyes fixed to mine, never flickering below my waist.

"I knew if I called, you'd tell me not to come. I had to make sure you were fine."

"I'm fine," I tell her, not stopping. I take the steps two at a time, headed into the house.

"You're also naked," she calls after me. "Did you realize?"

Little brat.

I grin. Nora glances up at me.

"Is it okay that I'm here, or?"

"Of course," I assure her. There's a whole lot of self-doubt in her eyes right now, and I want to squash it. "It's fine."

We get dressed quickly, then join Jacey in the kitchen. She's sitting at the kitchen table waiting for us, running her hand over the wood of the tabletop.

"I miss this cottage," she muses. "There were happy memories here."

And I had been in the process of making another one, but I don't point that out.

"Jacey, this is Nora Greene. Nora, this is Jacey Vincent. Kinkaide, I mean."

Nora holds out her hand, but Jacey by-passes it, hugging her instead.

"It's nice to meet you. So nice to meet you," Jacey gushes. "I feel like I know you, but that's not possible, right?"

"Her parents own the Greene estate," I interject helpfully and Jacey's eyes widen.

"Ohhhh. You're little Nora Greene! I knew I knew you. I used to wait tables at The Hill. I remember you coming in sometimes with your parents. You've...uh... grown up."

That's a tactful way to skirt around the topic that Nora was naked on Jacey's beach.

Nora smiles gracefully, only the barest hint of a blush along her pale cheeks.

"It's nice to meet you, Jacey. I've heard so much about you."

There's the barest hint of acid in her voice, and I wonder at it. Is she jealous?

Jacey looks at me, her brown eyes soft. "I couldn't help but notice, as I drove down this road, that your parents' house seems to have burned down."

There's a knowing expression on her face, because she knows me well.

I nod. "Yeah. There was a bit of a matches and gasoline problem. Apparently, when you douse something with gasoline and toss a match onto it, it burns."

She raises her eyebrow. "Is the problem resolved now?"

I nod. "It's all good."

"Good." Jacey yawns widely, then slaps a hand over her mouth. "God, I'm sorry. I'm jetlagged. Dom's still on-set in the UK and he couldn't come, but I wanted to be here for a couple of days to check on you. The jetlag is killing me, though. I'm gonna nap for a couple of hours, then we'll catch up, okay?"

"Of course," I tell her. "Take all the time you want. You can sleep in your old room. Nora's been sleeping in with me, anyway."

Jacey smiles knowingly. "I bet. I'll see you in a couple of hours." She heads down the hall, but calls over her shoulder.

"Don't think I'm not pissed that you didn't call me yourself. I'll be kicking your ass after I wake up."

"I'm scared!" I yell at her back.

The click of her bedroom door is my only answer. I look down at Nora, only to find her staring up at me. I can't read her expression.

"I'm sorry we were interrupted," I murmur into her hair, pulling her close. "But I'll make it up to you tonight."

She nods, but stays quiet. Her uncharacteristic silence is getting to me.

Jacey sleeps for hours, and in fact, I don't hear her stirring until long after Nora and I have gone to bed.

I lay in the dark, listening to Jacey's movements in the living room, and ponder my situation.

A year ago, I would've given anything to get Jacey to see me for me…. A grown man in love with her.

But things have changed, and the only thing I feel at the moment is annoyance, that her arrival has triggered doubts in Nora.

Because I saw the doubts in Nora's eyes. I saw that she questioned my feelings for Jacey, that those doubts caused her to question my feelings and my intentions for her.

We'll hang out with Jacey for a few days, but I'm going to have a talk with Nora. I know she wanted me for the summer, but I'm not cut out for that. Gran was right… when I open myself up to someone, I'm in it for the long haul.

The summer won't be enough.

Chapter Twenty-Three

Nora

I wake up to laughter and an empty bed.

Brand is gone, and as I glance out the bedroom windows, I see why. He's sitting at the picnic table in the sun, eating breakfast with Jacey.

I feel the early stirrings of jealousy in my belly and I fight to tamp them down. I don't own him. He's not mine. But he sleeps with me at night, he holds me all night long. I don't have anything to be jealous of.

That's what I tell myself.

It's hard though. Jacey keeps laying her hand on his arm, and they keep laughing over jokes I don't know. There's a familiarity between them that comes from years of knowing each other. *Really* knowing each other. It's hard not to be jealous of that.

Even though, at the same time, Jacey isn't throwing herself at him. Maybe she did at one point, but now, today, there doesn't seem to be sexual tension there at all.

I pull some clothes on, and run a brush through my hair, then join them outside with a cup of coffee.

"I wasn't sure how strong you like your coffee," Jacey tells me, looking up from their conversation. "So I just made it pretty mild. I hope that's fine."

"It's perfect," I assure her. I glance at the table, trying to decide which side to sit on. Jacey solves that problem by patting the bench next to her.

"Come tell me all about you," she sings cheerfully. "I've got to know all about the girl who has Brand intrigued."

He sighs loudly, but doesn't try and steer her away, so I sit down next to her.

We chat for the next hour.

Where do you live?

What do you do?

Where did you go to school?

The entire time, I find myself wishing that I was at Brand's side instead of Jacey's but I smile politely and chat and play the game. Because it's a game. I know it and Jacey knows it.

She's acting friendly and cheerful, but she's also acting on Brand's behalf. She's searching my motives, trying to decide if I'm good enough for her friend.

But she has no right.

She hurt him more than anyone else ever will.

But I keep a smile pasted on and I answer every question.

I even ask a few of my own.

What's it like being married to Dominic Kinkaide?

Where do you live now when you aren't on set with him?

Do you miss Angel Bay?

She answers my questions for the same reason as I answer hers.

A show for Brand.

It's when my phone buzzes in my pocket and I see William's name that I remember that I've got bigger problems to face than Jacey today.

Don't be late.

That's all he says. I glance at the time. It's already twelve-thirty. The knowledge that I need to go soon makes me uneasy. I don't want to leave them alone. But that's stupid, I tell myself. Brand is as loyal as they come.

But he's not mine.

That's an unarguable fact. He's no one's.

I swallow and look at the two of them.

"I'm sorry, but I've been summoned to work for a little bit. I have to drive into Chicago. I'll be back this evening though."

I get up to walk into the house, ignoring Brand's very concerned expression. Before I reach the door, his strong hand is gripping my elbow.

"Is everything ok?" he asks quickly, his blue eyes searching mine for an answer. An honest answer. I paste on a mask.

"Yes."

Lie.

He raises an eyebrow and I sigh.

"It's fine. My father just wants to give me some case files to study over the summer. He wants me to be prepared for the Fall."

Lie.

But I sound oh-so-convincing and Brand finally relaxes.

"Do you want me to ride along?"

Yes.

But I shake my head. "Of course not. You have company. Stay here with Jacey and catch up. I'll be home tonight."

Home.

A lump forms in my throat because this isn't my home. It's their home... Jacey's and Brand's. This is where they grew up. I'll never be a part of that.

"If you're sure...." Brand's voice trails off and I kiss him hard, on the mouth. Out of my periphery, I see Jacey watching us, something that gives me great satisfaction.

"I'm sure. I'll be back tonight."

I stride into the house with purpose and grab my purse. I don't look back until I'm all the way down the road.

***

The drive to Chicago seems to take forever, even though it's only an hour. I weave my Jag through the Sunday afternoon traffic and by the time I pull into my parking slot in the garage at Greene Corp, my nerves are shot.

My fingers are shaky, my heart is racing, my palms are clammy.

Brand and Jacey might be alone right now and that might be annoying, but I have to be alone with William. And that's more than annoying. It very well might be dangerous.

I gulp as I ride the elevator to the twentieth floor.

I swallow hard as I step out and my heels click on the polished floor.

Then, as I stand outside the doors of the conference room, I take a deep breath and try to steady myself. I know he's already here. I can smell his cologne on the air... something thick and cloying and old-man-like.

The smell brings back memories... of clawing and biting and penetration.

I gag a little bit, grabbing the wall.

I can do this.

I can do this.

This is me ringing the bell.

I open the door, and as confidently as I can, I step inside.

William waits for me at the far end of the massive conference table.

"Come in, my dear," he calls. Even his voice sounds like an old man, thin and frail. I swallow my disgust and approach him, keeping my eyes carefully on him as I stop across the table from him.

He smiles.

"Now, was this so hard? Really, my dear, meeting with me didn't have to be this way."

"I know what meeting with you is like," I manage to bite. "Why did you want to see me today? Let's just cut to the chase."

William nods, satisfied. "You're such a Greene, Nora. So ready to do what you need to do."

My stomach rolls.

"What do you want?" I ask stiltedly. My fingers are gripping the edge of the table so tightly that I can't feel them anymore.

William rocks back in his chair.

"I want to tell you a little bit about your boyfriend, of course. You're so young and inexperienced... I know you probably didn't do a background check on him. Right?"

I roll my eyes. "That's what you've got? I don't need a background check. I know him. He's a decorated Army Ranger, a hero who saved my life. That's all I need to know."

William chuckles, a thin fake sound in the quiet room. "Oh, my dear, you're so naïve. Your boyfriend *is* an Army Ranger. But I doubt he told you why."

I can tell from William's voice that I'm not going to like what he's going to say next. I wish I could close my ears and not listen, but I have to know.

William won't give me a choice.

I don't say anything, so he continues.

"Branden Killien attacked his father right after he graduated high school," William says with satisfaction, his faded eyes gleaming. "His parents pressed charges and the judge suspended the sentence if Branden would agree to join the military."

I'm stunned.

I'm not mad at Brand, because honestly, after hearing about his father and seeing his mother in action, I don't blame him. In fact, I commend him for waiting so long. But I am surprised that he didn't mention it.

William enjoys the look on my face.

"I see he didn't mention it to you," he says cheerfully. "I can see why. He thinks his records are sealed, so he never had to worry about telling you the truth. But see, my dear, nothing is sealed to me. I have connections everywhere. Which brings me to my point today."

He pauses and I wait. I stare him down, my gaze unflinching.

Fuck you, you fucking monster.

"I'm sure Brand doesn't want it known that the only reason he ever served his country was as a punishment for assault and battery. His company is successful in large part because of his and his partner's decorated military history. The connections I have in the pentagon... they wouldn't be very happy to know that they're doing business with a fraud."

My head snaps up.

"Brand isn't a fraud," I spit. "No one would ever think so."

William nods, very happy with my reaction, happy that he's getting one.

"They would believe that if I told them to. They would publicly withdraw their business and cite their reasons... that Branden is a fraud, a *criminal*, if I told them to. And when that happens, Brand's company would go bankrupt. He'd be ruined and left with nothing."

My breath leaves my body in a rush, even though I desperately try not to show it. "They wouldn't," I say, attempting to call his bluff. "His company does a good job. They would have no reason."

William drums his fingers casually on the table, as if we're having a friendly, normal conversation.

"My dear," he says, ever-so-sweetly. "They would do anything I ask them to do. That's how much weight I pull in Washington."

I stare at him and his eyes narrow as he gets up and walks toward me.

I have to fight to remain still, to stand my ground.

"You can't run from me."

He takes another step toward me, then another.

"I always get what I want."

He stops right in front of me, close enough that I have to breathe in his hateful cologne, and smell his fetid, hot breath.

"Ask me, Nora."

I turn my gaze up to meet his. His eyes are as cold as they are faded and old.

I seal my lips, unwilling to do it.

"Ask. Me."

He grabs one of my hands and squeezes it, pushing the delicate bones of my hands together. I grit my teeth with the pain.

He squeezes harder.

"What do you want?" I finally ask, to make him quit hurting me.

"You."

I fight the urgent need to vomit.

"He's getting in the way of what I want," William says pleasantly now, releasing my hand. "I want you to leave his cottage, and come with me for a trip to Abu Dhabi. We'll say it's for business. But I assure you, it won't be business."

His hand juts out and cups my crotch, his fingernails digging into my tender flesh there, biting into me. He likes pain. I know this. I've experienced it before. He likes *inflicting* pain.

I step backward, yanking away from him, from his evil touch.

"You don't want me. You wanted my mother and you couldn't have her. I'm not my mother."

William's wrinkled mouth pulls into a cynical smile. "What a clever girl you are. It might've started out that way, I wanted you because your mother had to watch me chase you and she could never do anything about it because she's a helpless cunt. But I want *you* now. Your mother is old."

So are you. I swallow the acid on my tongue.

"And if I say no?"

William raises a bushy eyebrow, as if he knows I'd never dare.

"If you said no, you'd be a very foolish girl. I'll ruin your meat-headed boyfriend, then I'll ruin you. And don't for one minute think that at least you'd have each other… because after I'm finished with him, he'll never want you. Not ever. Do you think he'd really want someone who willingly entered into an incestuous affair with her very own uncle and enjoyed it so much?"

Bile rises into my throat as he pulls out a pack of pictures and shoves them across the table.

It's me. Giving my own uncle a blow job.

From the angle of the camera, you can't see that my hands are bound behind my back. All you can see is the tattoo on my shoulder, a unique identifier. The twisted anchor, the words. *Fluctuat nec mergitur.* It's most definitely me.

And it's most definitely my uncle. His wrinkled hand is on the back of my head, forcing me to take more of him in my throat… and his very unique signet ring is on his finger.

My uncle smiles pleasantly as he tucks the pictures back in his pocket.

"There's more. There are many of you fucking me, you little whore," he tells me, each word icy. "And I don't care if it gets out... you were of legal age and if anyone questions me, I'll simply say that you're a wanton whore who pursued me for years and in a moment of drunkenness, I gave in to you. If you look at the pictures, it certainly appears that you're enjoying yourself."

I wasn't.

I wasn't enjoying myself. I was trying to get through it, to not die on the inside.

But he's right. You can't see that on the pictures. In the pictures, my make-up looks smeared from passion, not from tears. You can't see how my hands are bound, you can't see the lash-marks from my uncle's whip.

You can't see any of it... except for a girl having sex with her own uncle.

William stares at me, very sure that I'll be compliant. "Even if Brand still wanted you somehow after I ruin him," he says calmly. "He'll never want you after he sees what a fucked up slut you are."

Reality crashes down around me, ugly and hot.

No one in their right mind would want me after seeing those pictures.

No matter how I look at it, I'll lose Brand.

But I can't let Brand lose everything... not because of me. He's worked too hard to forget his own ugly past. It wouldn't be fair if he lost everything now.

"You have until midnight tomorrow night to leave that cottage," my uncle says pleasantly. "I'll meet you at your apartment in California. I know you kept it, even after your father said to let it go. It doesn't matter. It'll come in handy for us. We'll put it to good use until our flight leaves from LAX for Abu Dhabi."

I can't control my vomit.

I lean to the side and heave, over and over. I empty my stomach, then stand up again, wiping my mouth with my hand.

"I see we have an understanding," William nods. "Good. I'll see you in California, my dear."

He turns and starts to leave, but I stop him.

"What kind of monster are you?" I whisper. "I'm your flesh and blood. You held me when I was a baby. You're the criminal, not Brand."

William actually laughs, but it's hardened and ugly. "Nora, you and I both know you tried to seduce me from the time you were small. Those bathing suits you used to wear... you always made a point of walking away from me in a way that showed off your tight little ass."

Bile bubbles up again. "My ass was little because I was a child," I spit. "I never tried to seduce you. You're a sick fuck who preys on children."

William stares at me innocently. "I have never preyed on children," he defends himself. "I didn't have my way with you until you were an adult, my dear. That's not a crime."

"No, but it's an abomination," I tell him, all the while fighting the nausea again.

"To each their own," William says easily. "You have until midnight tomorrow night to leave for California. Don't be late."

He turns and strides from the room and I can still feel where his fingernails cut into my vagina. I rush to the bathroom and run a handful of paper towels under scalding hot water. I can't take a shower so this is the next best thing. I seclude myself in a bathroom stall, wiping and wiping and wiping, trying to get his finger prints off.

Before I realize it, I'm sobbing, and I'm in a heap on the floor.

I have until midnight tomorrow night with Brand.

I don't dare defy William.

He'll ruin everything I have. He'll bring my entire world down around me in shreds and tatters, but that's not what I care about.

All that I care about is…. Brand.

I can't let him hurt Brand.

I glance at my watch.

Time is ticking.

The shoe has dropped.

Chapter Twenty-Four

Brand

I stare at Jacey.

"What did you say?"

She swallows her bite of sandwich. "I said, what are you doing with this girl?"

I roll my eyes. "Not really your business, now is it? When it gets to a point that I think I need to tell you about it, you'll be the first to know."

"In other words," she scowls. "Never."

I grin.

She takes another bite. "She's gorgeous, I'll give you that. But she doesn't really seem your type. She's a bit... tightly wound."

I shake my head and look out at the lake, remembering how Nora has swam with me out to the buoy. "You think?"

Jacey nods. "She's from a snobby family, too. So not your type."

I finish up my sandwich and take my plate to the sink. "Jacey, no offense. But you've spent years crying on my shoulder over other men. You haven't once listened to me talking about a woman. You don't know my type."

She stops chewing and stares at me. "Never once?"

I shake my head. "Never once. I was always listening to you."

"God, I was a bitch," she mutters. "Should I apologize again?"

I roll my eyes. "Nah. It won't help now. Just know that I know what I'm doing. And if I want your advice, I'll ask for it. And thank you for letting me use your cottage to recuperate."

She scowls good-naturedly. "Is that what you're calling it? Recuperation? In a cottage alone with a beautiful woman?"

I nod. "It's my story."

"And you're sticking to it. Got it."

We banter back and forth for a while, and Jacey chats about life in the UK and I tell her all about what her brother's been up to in Connecticut.

"This is nice," she finally says, leaning up to hug me. "I feel like things are back to where they should be. Finally. I'm sorry for fucking it all up in the first place."

"It's fine," I tell her as I hug her back. "Seriously."

Before Jacey can pull away, the door opens and Nora steps in.

Of course. Because Jacey still has her arms wrapped around me. Perfect.

The look on Nora's face is chilling.

I step away from Jacey immediately, and reach for Nora.

"Hey, sweetheart," I greet her. "Jacey and I were just catching up."

Nora nods slowly, not smiling. "I see that."

Jacey looks from Nora to me. "Uh. I need to go in to the Hill and see Maria. I'll be back later. My flight takes off in the morning, so I'll need to get some sleep."

Neither Nora or I answer, so Jacey slips away.

I stare at Nora.

"That wasn't what it looked like."

"No?" Nora's eyebrow is arched.

"No." I shake my head. "It was just a hug between friends."

Nora stares at me for a moment, her eyes big and sad. Then she nods, the clouds clearing from her face. "Okay."

"Okay? Just like that?"

She nods. "Just like that. I trust you. And there's better ways to spend my time than to be suspicious of you."

"Babe, we've always got time to talk about shit. If you feel bad about something, you need to tell me. That's how people sort things out. Time is cheap. We can afford it."

She stares at me sadly and for a minute, I'm bothered. What the hell is with her?

But then she smiles.

"You're right. But I'm fine. Jacey is an old friend. It's fine."

It's fine. Two of the most dangerous words in the female vocabulary, I'm sure. But I have no other choice than to accept it. So I nod.

"Good. Now… we have the cottage to ourselves again for the evening. How would you like to spend *that* time?"

Nora smiles, a slow smile that finally reaches her eyes, then she reaches for me.

"I've got some ideas."

***

Nora

I've got to soak him up. Every bit of him, as much as I can. I've got so little time to absorb him, to remember him, to take his goodness and make it mine.

He runs his hands over my hips, and I lift them, granting him access to the most sensitive part of me. When he does, I forget how William's fingernails bit into me earlier. Brand eclipses it, erases it, eradicates it.

I twist the sheets in my hand, moaning his name as he strokes me.

Make me good, Brand.

He kisses my neck, my lips, my cheeks, before he rests his forehead against mine and as he stares into my eyes, he enters my body, slowly, smoothly, deeply.

With purpose.

I suck in my breath and then breathe with him, in slow pants as he slides in and out, over and over.

"I want to see you," he rasps against my neck. And then he pulls out, and flips me on top of him, his hands grasping my breasts, kneading the sensitive flesh.

"That's better," he sighs. Sliding his hands along my hips, he worships them. Then he spends his attention on my breasts and leaning up, he suckles them, laving them with his tongue, rolling my nipples between his teeth. All the while, I'm rocking on his hardness, sliding him in and out, enjoying the wet warmth, the hardened rigidity.

Fill me up, Brand.

He slides in and out, fast then faster and finally, I throw my head back and arch on top of him, shattered from the orgasm. I shake and shake with it, my muscles contracting around him.

He smiles.

"My turn."

He begins moving inside of me again, but then pulls out, and flips me over one more time, this time, I'm face-down on the bed as he fucks me from behind. He pulls me up toward him with his hands and then reaches around and strokes me while he fucks me.

I come again, before he finally groans with his own release.

I collapse onto the bed, limp and satisfied and sad.

This is all I have. I have to memorize it. I have to memorize him, his face, his smell, his hands.

I pick up one of his hands and trace his fingers as he pulls me onto his chest with his other arm.

The silence between us is huge and loaded and important. I don't know why. Then I realize... as he looks at me, the expression in his eyes is different.

Because he loves me.

I don't know how I know, but I know.

I nuzzle into him, my face in his neck, trying to spread that warm, soft, *good* feeling all over my body.

"I'm so tired," I tell him, hoping that he won't actually say the words. I can't hear the words. Not if I have to leave him. It'd be impossible. Excruciating.

Please don't.

He chuckles instead and the moment is broken. "I wore you out. Take a nap and we'll do it again."

But he's the one who falls asleep.

I watch him, as he breathes in and out. As his arms still encircle me, as he still protects me even while he sleeps.

My heart twinges, my gut tightens.

I glance at the clock.

Eleven pm.

We've spent hours in this bedroom, making love over and over. Because that's how I wanted to spend my last hours with him. It will be these memories that I exist on from this day forward.

But the clock is ticking and I have one hour. I have no doubt that William probably has someone watching the house, just to make sure I hold up my end of the bargain.

As gently as I can, I slip from the bed and sit at the desk by the window, scribbling out a note. It's brief but I don't know what else to say... I don't know what to say that won't hurt him. I fold it over and write Brand's name on it, propping it up by the lamp where he'll see it.

I watch him again, soaking him in, memorizing his strong face, his chiseled jaw, the cleft in his chin. I wish I could look into his eyes one more time... the blue, blue ocean that I've looked into a hundred times.

The eyes that say they love me, even if he hasn't said the words. I know he does. I saw it tonight.

And that will have to be enough.

I bend and brush the softest of kisses on his brow and slip from the room.

I know Jacey isn't back yet, so I quickly grab my things from her room, stuffing them in my bag. I'm quietly walking through the kitchen when the back door opens and Jacey steps in.

She's startled to see me and she starts to say hello, but then her eyes take in the bag in my hand and widen.

"Are you... you're leaving."

I swallow hard, then nod. The movement hurts, like a scalpel or a sword.

"And Brand doesn't know."

Jacey's voice is limp.

I stare at her, not answering.

She stares back, confused, pissed.

I take a step around her and she grabs my elbow.

"I don't know if this matters to you, but I haven't seen Brand this happy in a long time. Actually, I've never seen him this happy. This will kill him. I can't imagine why you'd leave him."

I stare at her, directly in the eyes.

"You left him."

"But he and I were never together," she points out. "You... I ... never mind. It's not my business."

She turns her back and starts to walk away.

"Jacey?"

She turns around silently, because words aren't needed. Her icy glare says everything.

"Sometimes things aren't what they seem. Can you.. just... take care of him."

Jacey nods curtly, one time, and I do the hardest thing I'll ever have to do in my life.

I drive away from Brand Killien.

I sob the entire way to the airport.

Chapter Twenty-Five

Brand

When I wake, the bed is empty. It takes a minute to realize that Nora has already gotten up. I stretch and wait for her to come back, but after a long while passes, I realize she's not going to.

She must be out talking with Jacey.

I shake my head as I climb from bed. What a fucked up situation. But what an amazing night.

As I reach for my shorts, I see the paper.

Folded over, with my name scrawled on it, propped up on the desk. My stomach drops like a piece of lead, into my feet, into the floor.

This can't be good.

I don't want to open it, but at the same time, I know I have to.

My body goes numb as I read her words.

Brand,
This was more than I bargained for. I'm sorry. I hope you find what you're looking for.

Nora

She doesn't mean it.
She can't possibly.
Yet, she's gone. And this letter is here in her place.

I ball the paper up and throw it in the trashcan and then before I can control my anger, I smash my fist into the wall. It breaks through the drywall with a crash, and little pieces of it fall to the floor.

It doesn't take Jacey long to come running.

"Jesus," she breathes, taking in my bloody knuckles and the hole in the wall. "I'll get a washcloth."

She disappears and comes back within a minute, forcing me to sit on the bed and pressing the wet cloth around my hand. "I'll pay for the repairs," I mumble.

"I don't care about the wall," she tells me. "I care about you. Are you going to be ok?"

I growl and look away. "Of course. This isn't the first time I haven't been good enough for someone."

Jacey sucks in a breath and looks at me, her eyes wide and blue and hurt.

"I'm sorry," I mutter. "I'm not mad at you. I'm just...fuck."

Jacey rubs my back, her head on my shoulder. "I don't know what to say. I'm sorry, Brand."

"This is bullshit," I tell her as I stand up. "It doesn't make any sense."

But it makes all kinds of sense.

No one stays with me. For as long as I've been alive, I've never been fucking good enough. It doesn't matter how good I am, how strong I get, how good a job I do... it's never enough.

Not for anyone.

"Fuck this."

I stride from the room, intent on going somewhere, anywhere... to get this shit out of my head.

Everything is swirling through my thoughts... my father who beat me, my mother who hates me, Jacey who didn't want me... and now Nora. It all bleeds together and I can't tell the emotions apart.

I'm simply not good enough.

As I walk through the living room, my eyes fall on that fucking wooden box and I pick it up, gripping it tight. It just symbolizes one more failure.

Jacey trails behind me and stares at it. "What's that?"

"I wasn't good enough to save my little sister," I tell her, my voice sharp, the words painful. "Did you know that?"

Jacey shakes her head, her eyes wide. "I didn't know you had a sister," she answers softly.

I nod. "Yeah. I did. She drowned when I was six and I wasn't good enough to stop it. At least, that's what my old man always told me... when he was beating the shit out of me every night. Those bruises I had when I was a kid? That's why I got them. Because I wasn't fucking good enough."

Jacey is still, completely frozen. "My grandma called social services, you know," she tells me. "They came and investigated your father, but they couldn't find enough evidence to take you away."

Of course not. I vaguely remember that, too. One summer, when I was twelve or so, I'd come home for a change of clothes and there were people at the house, strange people in pant suits who asked a lot of questions. My father had stared meaningfully at me, and I'd answered them all like I know he'd want me to.

Kids are loyal to the end.

Well guess what? It's the end.

I grip the box hard, staring at it's intricate design, at the way it so cleverly conceals it's contents. Hard and fast, I throw it across the room. It shatters against the wall, splintering into pieces on the floor.

I don't make a move to walk to it, to see what's inside.

Jacey stares first at it, then at me.

"I don't know what happened to your sister," she says softly. "But I do know that whatever it was, it wasn't your fault."

I can't help it. It all wells up in me and I sink to the floor and sit limply, and all of it comes out. All of it.

My sister sleepwalking. The way we had to keep her locked in for her own safety. How my mother had found her washed up on the shore and how her screams had shaken the house. How my father had beat me every night when he came home from the bar. *Ring the bell, Brand.* How he had swung at me when I graduated high school and how then it was my turn to beat him. How I'd punched him and punched him until my mother pulled me off and called the police. How the judge had suspended my sentence when he heard I'd been accepted to West Point, but only if I'd agree to enter the military afterward. How that was okay with me, because it's had been my plan anyway. And how my mother hates me now.

All of it comes out.

All of it.

Jacey holds my hand and tears stream down her face as she listens to me rail and vent and swear. Years of disgust and bitterness flow out of me, all of it.

All.

Of.

It.

Even the parts that are directed at her.

"You used me for years," I tell her angrily. "And I let you. That's on me. Because I always thought I wasn't good enough.. it's something that's embedded deep down--- so I always felt like that's what I deserved. To take and take and take. Well you know what? Fuck that. I don't deserve that."

Jacey grips my hand tighter.

"No, you don't deserve that, Brand. And you were always good enough. Always. I was the one who wasn't good enough for *you*. Your dad was asshole. Your mother is just as bad. They fucked you up, but you're stronger than they are. You are. You're good and strong and loyal... and you were more of a man when you were six than your father was ever. You have to know that, Brand. You have to."

I'm finally done railing. I'm limp and tired and exhausted.

I nod. "Yeah. I do know that. I've spent my entire life trying to be *good enough*. I think it's time that I just... that I just *am*."

Jacey nods and holds me and I close my eyes for just a minute.

"I didn't deserve for Nora to leave in the middle of the night without even a conversation. Fuck her."

My eyes pop open and Jacey is watching me, her face pale.

"I'm going to shower," I tell her as I get up. And I walk away.

A minute later, though, Jacey calls me.

I hesitate at my bedroom door.

"Yes?" I call back.

"I looked in the box."

Her words are simple, her tone calm.

Suddenly, I want to know. What the fuck did my father have to say? What could he *possibly* have to say to me?

I stride back to the living room and find Jacey standing over the shattered remains of the box. She turns to look at me, her face pale, her eyes huge.

There, dangling from her fingers, is the old sliding lock from my sister's bedroom door.

The paint is peeling from it, it's old and it's rusty, but it's as familiar to me as my own hand. If I close my eyes, I can still hear the sound it made when it slid into place every night before bed.

If I close my eyes, and imagine the sound, I also know something, something that I've purposely not thought about over the years, but something I've known since the night my sister died.

I didn't hear the lock slide into place that night.

It's something I've never told another living soul.

Jacey stares at me.

I stare at the lock.

"I knew my father didn't lock Allison's door that night," I finally say. "I knew. I waited until he left for the bar, and I snuck downstairs for a snack, for some cookies. I meant to lock the door when I went back to bed, but I forgot. I walked right past and I forgot. I laid in bed that night, staring out my window, staring at what I thought was a silver ball floating away in the water."

I pause, and the silence is pregnant as Jacey waits.

"It wasn't a ball," I say starkly. "It was my sister."

Jacey's eyes widen a bit more, but she remains silent.

"So all along, my parents were right. I guess that's why I always felt like I deserved whatever my father gave me," I admit, my words wooden. "I knew her door wasn't locked and I forgot to do anything about it. She's dead and it's as much my fault as it is anyone's."

The guilt, the guilt that I've carried my entire life feels like a weight now, a heavy weight, an albatross of iron around my neck.

I glance at Jacey. "So now you know. Everyone has been right all along. I'm just not good enough."

There are tears streaking down Jacey's face now and she drops the lock. It makes a heavy thump as it hits the floor and Jacey rushes to me, burying her face in my chest as she cries. But she's not seeking comfort for once. This time, she's the one comforting me.

"Brand, you're amazing. So, so amazing. You were six years old. There's no way that you could've known that your sister would get up that night. It wasn't your responsibility to make sure that door was locked. It was your parents. People suck because they have to always find someone to blame for bad shit... someone besides themselves. You've been carrying this guilt for too long... and it's not yours to carry. It's your father's. And I think... maybe...this was his way of saying that."

I look down at her and she wipes at her eyes.

"Look." She points with a shaky hand at the inside of the wooden lid. Inscribed with perfect craftsmanship, the words stand out starkly.

It was me.

"I think he's finally trying to set you free."

The silence of the house is huge, reverent.

My father's guilt is not my burden anymore.

***

Because it stands a hundred yards away from the house, my father's woodshop was undamaged in the fire.

This morning, I stand in the doorway, assessing it. Distracting myself from the massive hole that Nora's absence has left.

She's gone.

I can't believe it, and I feel it in every part of me. Every cell in my body is in shock, every molecule screams with the pain.

Fuck it.

I take a few steps inside, picking up half finished pieces of wood. She's gone because I'm not enough for her. I'm not *good enough.*

The old feelings of inadequacy slam into me, again and again and I groan, slamming the wood in my hand into a table.

Fuck her.

I begin picking up all of my father's half-finished projects and taking them across the room, stacking them neatly in a corner. I'll discard them later. It takes a few loads because my father had tons of projects. But anything to keep my hands busy, anything to keep me from punching a million holes into the wall.

I pause and remember my father puttering around out here for hours on end. I used to hear the saws and be thankful... because it meant he probably wouldn't go to the bar that night. And if he didn't go to the bar and get trashed, then I was safe from his wrath. He only beat me when he was drunk.

As I reach for another handful of wood, I catch a glimpse of a red metal box sticking out from under the workbench. Bending, I pull it out, expecting to find tools. But no.

Inside the old toolbox, is a stack of papers. Newspapers, letters from West Point, clippings. All about me. The old man had been keeping tabs on me over the years. He knew I graduated from West Point, he knew I'd made the Rangers, he knew I'd been sent to Afghanistan. He even knew I'd earned a Purple Heart. He was too proud to contact me, but he cared enough to follow my life.

For a minute, my heart softens.

Life really isn't black or white.

Fuck life. It's a vengeful bitch.

I drop the box, stalk to the fridge in the corner and grab a beer. My father's got at least two cases left, chilled and ready for me. On second thought, I turn and grab two more, and then head for the chair at his desk. I put my feet up on the desk and lean my chair back, popping the top of beer number one. The other two are lined up waiting for me.

Yes, it's not even noon yet.

No, I don't give a flying fuck.

It's hot as hell in here, but I don't care about that, either. I just stare out the window as I gulp the cold brew down.

I don't care about my father's stash of newspaper clippings. I don't care about his fucking box or the way he finally took ownership of his own guilt.

All I care about is Nora.

Why in the name of all that's holy did I put myself in this position? I knew from the beginning that Nora only wanted the summer. That she only wanted me to fulfill some stupid fucking high school fantasy. I knew that.

Yet I got sucked in anyway.

Because I'm a stupid fuck and everything about her made me feel good.

Well, fuck that. I'm not feeling too good right now.

I crush the can and toss it to the side, picking up beer number two.

I crack the top.

"You gonna sit out here and drink all day?"

Jacey's voice comes from behind me. I take a gulp.

"That's the plan."

She walks softly around me, perching on the edge of the desk. She's still wearing shorts and flip-flops.

"Didn't you have a flight this morning?" I ask her, taking another long gulp.

She shakes her head. "I did. But I'm not going to leave you now."

I stare at her. "Uh-uh. Get on that plane, Vincent. I'm fine."

She shakes her head again. "Nope. You nursed me through five million break-ups. I can be here for one."

I down the beer and reach for number three.

"Nope. I honestly don't want you here, Jace. I love you and all, but I think I need to be alone. I'm going to be an asshole for a few days. You don't need to be here for that."

She starts to protest, to tell me how she's been a bitch around me before, yada, yada, yada, but I cut her short, leveling a gaze at her.

"Seriously, Jacey. I appreciate it. But go back to your husband. I need to be alone."

She opens her mouth, then closes it. She stares at me for the longest time, before finally nodding.

"I guess. If that's what you want." She takes a few steps toward the door, then turns. "Brand, one of the very best things about you is your heart. You could've turned out to be an asshole in life, because of all the shit you dealt with as a kid, but you didn't. You turned out to be the absolute best man I know. Don't let any of this change that. Please."

I snort, lifting can number three to my lips.

"Whatever, Jace. Look where it got me. Nice guys finish last. Every. Fucking. Time."

I turn my back on her, looking out the window as I gulp the brew down. At this rate, I very well might go through a case today. And that's fine.

I hear Jacey behind me, lingering, trying to decide what to say. It annoys the fuck out of me.

"Just go, Jacey," I tell her firmly. "Seriously. Have a safe flight."

She flies back to me, throwing herself at me, hugging me tight. Her arms clamp around my throat and I have to pry them off so I can breathe.

"What the hell?"

She glances up at me, her eyes watery. "I'm sorry she hurt you, Brand. It sucks. I don't know why she left, but you deserve to be happy."

I look away. "Yeah. I do. But you know what they say…"

"What do they say?"

A voice comes from the doorway, a voice with a French accent.

Jesus. Do people not ever knock around here?

Camille Greene stands elegantly in the woodshop, as out of place among the dust and wood shavings as Maxwell had been on the porch.

She stares from Jacey to me, curiosity in her blue eyes, at the way Jacey is draped around my neck, but she doesn't say anything else.

"It doesn't matter what they say," I mutter, and I gently push Jacey off my lap. I stare at her, my expression firm.

"Go back to the UK. Go be with your husband. I'll be fine."

She nods. "Fine. But call me if you need me." She takes a step, then two, then turns around.

"I just have to say this one thing. I don't know her very well, but Nora didn't look like someone who wanted to leave, Brand. I don't know why else she would be leaving, but she didn't look like it was a choice she wanted to make."

This yanks my head up. "Why do you say that?"

Jacey shakes her head. "I can't explain it. It was just a look in her eyes."

A look in her eyes. Jesus. Leave it to a woman to say something like that.

Jacey turns and walks past Camille, who then steps further inside.

"I didn't mean to intrude," she tells me elegantly. "I'm sorry."

"How did you know to look for me in here?" I ask her curiously. She shrugs her slim shoulders.

"You weren't at the other cottage, and I knew this was your parents'. So I came looking."

I stare at her, at her silk pantsuit and her perfectly coiffed hair, her jewels, her expensive taste.

"Why?"

My question is as stark as I feel.

She returns my gaze without flinching.

"Because I agree with your friend. My daughter has run away, and I don't think she wanted to. And I need your help to get her back."

For just one second, I feel hope rise inside of me, but then I snort and turn away, because I remember why Nora ran away.

"She ran from *me*," I answer coldly, getting up and walking toward the fridge again. I unload three more beers into my arms before I walk back. "Because I'm not what she wants, and she didn't want to be here anymore. So I won't be of much help in finding her."

Camille steps forward and puts her hand on my arm. It's slender and cool and I look at her. Her face is pained, worried. From here, I can see that she's tired. Like she didn't sleep much.

"Nora texted me in the middle of the night," Camille continues, like I'd not spoken at all. "It was very strange. I know you know that all is not right in my family. I feel like I can trust you… that I can tell you this." She draws in a big breath.

"I told Nora once that if William ever hurt her, to come to me instead of her father. Because there are things she doesn't know. Maxwell isn't... well, it doesn't matter right now. But what does matter is that she texted me last night. This is what it said."

She pulls her phone from her purse, finds the text and hands it to me.

Mom,

You were right. William is a monster. But I'm going to do something about it. You might not see me for a while. But I love you. Don't worry. Either way, everything is finally going to be ok.

The words, so stark and formal, cut through me and send chills down my spine. It doesn't sound like Nora at all... unless she was desperate. And she sounds desperate.

What the fuck did I miss?

"What does she mean that she's going to do something about it?" Camille asks me in a whisper, her forehead furrowed and her fingers gripping my arm. "What is she going to do?"

I shake my head slowly from side to side, trying to wrap my mind around the words.

"I don't know what happened. She went to work yesterday... said she had to meet her father to go over case files. When she came back, she acted strange."

My voice trails off, but Camille is already shaking her head. "She didn't meet Maxwell yesterday. He was at the house. All day."

We look at each other and Camille is already pulling out her phone.

She punches in a number, then waits. "Hello? Darleen? It's Camille. Darling, I can't get a hold of William. Is he traveling?"

She pauses.

"He's flying out of San Francisco for Dubai? On the company jet?"

A pause.

"Okay. Is he the only traveler listed on the flight manifest?"

Another pause, and her eyes meet mine.

"Okay. Well, I'll just call Nora then. Thank you, Darleen."

She pushes end and I can see her finger shaking.

"What's wrong?"

She looks at me again. "William and Nora are taking the corporate jet to Dubai this evening. It was supposed to fly out this afternoon, but there's been some sort of delay at the airport. Something about the flight patterns, etc. That's not important. The important thing is that Nora is leaving with William. There's no reason that she would do that, unless somehow, he's making her."

My stomach drops and the hair rises on the back of my neck as I remember the way William watched Nora at the dinner party, at the way his eyes undressed her. It gives me chills even now.

Camille puts her hand on mine. "Please. I know you care about Nora. I know it because I can see it. She didn't leave you willingly. I feel it. I know it. William is an evil man. Nora is... she feels trapped in her life, helpless to change it. But I know things that can free her. Please. She won't answer her phone. Can you help me get to her? I have a feeling she's planning something... dire."

The wording of her text is strange. *Either way, everything is finally going to be ok.*

Either way *what?*

I nod. "Okay. I'll help. But San Francisco is a big place. We can't possibly know where they'll be until their plane takes off."

Camille shakes her head. "I know exactly where they'll be. San Francisco is thirty minutes from Nora's apartment. She kept it, even though her father told her to let it go. She told me that she needed a place of her own, a place where she can be alone. There is no *good* reason that she would take William to that apartment, but I know she is, even though she absolutely hates him. Even though she fears him. Darleen told me that William is already in California, far ahead of their departure time. So what in the world is going on between now and this evening?"

Camille's voice is rushed and cold and afraid.

And I know she's right. We've got to get there. Nora would never choose to be alone with William.

I know that as sure as I'm breathing.

She's been hiding something this week. Her attitude was fidgety, nervous, unsettled. I didn't know why.

A sense of urgency presses against me, and my instincts roar to life, even through the haze of the beer. Something is very wrong and all she'd said was *it's fine.*

My instincts had been right. She's not fine.

She was lying.

I pull out my phone and try to call her, but it goes instantly to voicemail.

"Nora, call me when you get this. It's important."

I look at Camille. "Let's go."

She nods and takes my arm. "Greene Corp has a second jet at O'Hare. We can use it."

My heart pounds against my ribs as we tear down the road in Camille's Mercedes. Adrenaline pumps through me and I realize something with a start.

The reason I'm so devastated by Nora's leaving... is because I love her.

When we get to her, whether she still wants to leave me or not, I have to tell her. She needs to know, and I have to say the words.

I wanted to say them last night, and something held me back. And if I can't get to her today, she'll never know.

I'll have to live knowing that the beautiful, seemingly confident girl who secretly feels worthless doesn't know I love her... she doesn't know that she's more valuable than anything on the face of the earth.

William Greene had better pray to any God that will listen that he hasn't harmed a hair on her head.

Chapter Twenty-Six

Nora

My blood is chilled in my veins as I open the door to my apartment and look around.

Nothing is disturbed. Everything is exactly the way I left it when I packed for Angel Bay a few weeks ago.

The apartment is still cozy and neat and clean. Not fancy, but perfect for me. It was all I needed when I went through law school. I could've lived here forever.

Leaving my front door unlocked, I set my bag down by the kitchen table and sink into a chair, my head in my hands.

How has everything changed in so short a time?

A few weeks ago, I knew what my life was going to be like and even though I hated it, I was resigned to doing it. I'm a Greene, after all. I do what it fucking takes.

But then... there was Brand. And everything changed.

I can't keep doing this.

I can't.

I square my shoulders. My father has an iron-clad contract with my signature on it, tying me to him for the next twenty years. William has information on Brand that could ruin him... and *will* ruin him if I don't comply.

There's only one thing that I can do to survive.

I have to take care of William and then run.

I'll hide where my father can never find me.

It's all I can do.

All of a sudden, I feel a strange calm come over me and I feel as though I'm watching from afar, from outside of my body.

This isn't me, this isn't my life.

It'll all be over soon.

One way or another.

I get up and calmly walk to the bedroom.

Standing on my toes, I reach onto the top shelf of my closet and pull down a box.

Inside, a silver 9mm gleams in the light.

I never thought I'd have the balls to use it. I never thought I could.

But oh, how things change.

I run my finger over the cold metal before I lift it from the box and load it.

Very, very calmly, I take off my clothes and sit on my bed in only my black bra and panties. In the middle of the bed, I tuck my legs beneath me, and wait.

It'll all be over soon.

One way or another.

Out the window, I watch the ocean. It crashes against the shore, while sail boats and paddleboards ride the waves. Everyone out there is carefree and happy. Everyone out there is normal.

In here, I'm tainted and twisted and used.

But it all ends today.

Chapter Twenty-Seven

Brand

I stare down at the wings of the plane, as we descend through the clouds and toward the ground.

I can't focus on anything, other than Nora's face the other night.

Her eyes had been so wide, as she'd looked at me in the dark.   As I'd entered her, she'd sighed so soft, and then whispered into my neck.

Make me good, Brand.

Her words were so quiet that I don't even know that she meant to speak.

But the words twist and turn in my heart right now.

Make me good.

Because she thinks she's not. She thinks she's used.

Unworthy.

Because of whatever that fucking asshole has done to her.

Make me good, Brand.

I grit my teeth and squirm in my seat. I need to get to her. Now.

She's everything good in the world. She just doesn't know it.

And I will fucking annihilate him if he's touched her.

He'll beg for mercy.

And I will not give it to him.

Chapter Twenty-Eight

Nora

My spine is ram-rod straight as I wait.

As the clock ticks the minutes past.

The seconds.

The moments.

This summer, there just wasn't enough time with Brand. It all ticked past so fast. And now that I've left him, the seconds are coming so slowly, passing like razor blades on my skin, achingly, wretchedly slow.

I can do this.

I'm brave.

I'm brave.

I'm fucking brave.

Being brave doesn't mean not being afraid, Nora. It means being afraid and doing it anyway.

The mere memory of Brand's voice, his words, makes me smile, warms my heart and buoys my resolve.

How dare William threaten him?

I could've cowered forever under threats toward me, but toward Brand?

That's where they fucked up.

The front door opens. I hear the latch, I hear the knob. I lift my chin.

I'm fucking brave.

I'm fucking brave.

I reach under the edge of the mattress, my fingertips reaching, feeling. Cool metal answers my question. It's there... just within reach. Concealed and waiting.

It all ends today.

A polished loafer appears in my bedroom doorway, and I follow the legs up to the waist, up to the chest, up to the face where hardened brown eyes stare at me.

"Nora," my father says, a camera dangling from his hand. "I see you're ready."

He eyes me, all of me, my bare legs, my breasts spilling from my bra, my bare skin, my arms, my face. It's all exposed.

For my father and my uncle.

My reality slams into me, hard and fast and ugly.

I'm tainted.

I'm used.

But it all ends today.

One more time.

One.

More.

Time.

I unclench my teeth and lay back on the bed, spreading my legs the way they like.

"A Greene does what it takes," I tell my father coldly. "You taught me that."

My father nods, his gaze fixed on my crotch. He snaps a picture, then two, then three.

"Starting without me?"

William steps in. He's already shed his clothes, probably in the living room, and he's only wearing his underwear. He's pale, wrinkled, sagging. My stomach turns, but I ignore it.

I'm fucking brave.

"Take off your bra for your uncle, Nora," my father tells me, with eyes like a predator. "You know what he likes."

The camera snaps. Again. Then again.

Just like last time, my father stands in the corner, behind the camera, stroking himself while his brother gets off. Like last time, he'll be careful to stay out of the photos. He only takes them so that William can get off on them later.

William crawls onto the bed, on all fours, his white gut sagging to the sheets. I pull my legs up, away from his skin, not wanting to touch him.

I squeeze my eyes shut, preparing.

I can do this.

I'm fucking brave.

"Open your eyes, Nora," William breathes into my ear, his rank breath hot on my face. "I want to see you as I fuck you."

He moves over me, hovering, positioning, and I reach to the side, beneath the edge of the mattress. My fingers close around the cold steel.

That's when I open my eyes.

And that's when the breath freezes on my lips.

Bursting through the doorway, with all the fury of hell in his eyes, is my avenging angel.

Chapter Twenty-Nine

Brand

Rage settles down on me, like a cloud, like a shield, as I bellow my way into the room.

With one fist, I punch Maxwell Greene in the face, slamming him into the wall. In one deft motion, I ram my boot into his dick, crushing it. I leave him whimpering in a heap on the floor.

With one bound, I grab William by the neck and drag him from the bed, ramming his face into the wall, again, then again, then again.

I don't see, I don't hear, I don't feel.

I just *am*.

I just am enraged.

I'm a machine, intent on revenge, on protecting what is mine. I punch William until his face is a wet pulp. The anger pumps through my veins, pushing the rage through my heart, fueling me.

"Brand!"

Nora's voice breaks through the cloud and I pause, mid-punch, my fist frozen in the air. I turn and she's poised on the bed, a delicate waif, beautiful and haunting, and with a 9 mm pointed at William's chest.

"Stand back," she tells me calmly, her voice cold and soft.

I drop William and step back, my eyes frozen on her face.

William is unconscious on the floor, blood spurting from his mouth, and gurgling in his nose. Maxwell moans from behind him, his hands clasped to his broken cock.

"Nora," I speak softly, my eyes trained only on her. I see in her eyes that she means it. She's not aiming to maim.

She's aiming to kill.

"Nora, I know you're hurt. What they've done is unthinkable, but I don't want their blood on your hands. You don't know what that's like. You don't *deserve* to know what that's like. They can't hurt you now, Nora. We'll call the police. It will be over."

Nora keeps the gun on William's chest, but she looks at me, her eyes big and blue.

And cold.

"Brand, you don't understand," she says simply. "I can't get away from them. William will ruin you. He knows about your past... about assaulting your father and how the judge made you join the Army. He's going to use that to bankrupt your company — because he knows people in Washington. And my father..."

I speak up, trying as best I can to stay calm, to dissuade her. "Nora, they can't ruin me. I was always going to be a Ranger. It was my dream from the time I was a kid. I wanted to protect people from evil like my father. The judge knew that. The judge saw the situation for what it was and gave me a break. Nora, they can't hurt me."

But she's unmoved and her voice is filled with contempt.

"Don't you see? It doesn't matter what the truth is. William has connections in the pentagon who will believe whatever he tells them to. If he wants to ruin you, he'll ruin you. And that's not all. I signed a contract that ties me to my father for twenty years. I can't do that. I just can't. I've got to end it today, Brand. It ends today."

Her voice is so resigned that it sends my heart pounding into my throat, especially when I see her hand shaking. She means to do it.

She means it. I want to lunge and grab the gun from her, but I'm too afraid she'll hurt herself with it in the struggle. I can't risk it.

I eye her carefully, thinking through my options, but then Camille steps forward, her shocked and frozen face finally moving to speak.

"My baby," she croons, edging toward the bed. "There's so much that you need to know. Please... put down the gun. They can't hurt you now. They can't."

Nora shakes her head. "Step back, maman."

But Camille refuses. "Nora, you need to know something... something I've never been strong enough to tell you. Look at me."

Nora pauses, but doesn't look at her mother. She keeps the gun trained on William. "Just tell me."

Camille's tone is blunt. "Nora, you're not Maxwell's daughter. Your contract will be void, not that it ever mattered anyway."

This stops Nora cold, something that finally breaks through her concentration. She stares at her mother in confusion.

"Not his?" She looks at the two bloody men. "What do you mean?"

There's the smallest tone of hope hidden among her confusion.

Camille stares at her, with love and fear and apprehension.

"You aren't a Greene. Maxwell Greene is not your father. That means that the contract you signed, which named you as his daughter, isn't valid. He can't keep you with him. He can't force you to do anything ever again."

Nora's eyes fill and her lips shakes. "That's impossible. How..."

Camille shakes her head. "We'll talk about it more after you put the gun down, my love. Please. Just give Brand the gun. Everything is going to be ok. I promise. It will be okay. "

Each second seems to last a year as I watch Nora's hand shake while she clenches the gun, as she finally turns her gaze toward her mother. The cold, blank expression is gone, and instead, her eyes are filled with hope.

"If you're telling the truth... then...they aren't... William isn't...my uncle and...."

A tear breaks rank and slides down her cheek.

"I'm not..."

I speak up. "You're not *used*, Nora," I tell her quietly. "You never have been. What they did to you was sick and wrong. And we'll send them to prison because that's where they deserve to rot."

The gun shakes and drops to her side, and it's finally safe for me to step forward, closing my hand around the barrel, and easing it out of her hand.

She rests against me, sinking into my arms, her head against my chest.

"I hear your heart," she says slowly, and I know what she's doing. I've done it a thousand times in combat. She's removing herself from the situation. It's something a person does to survive, to block out the ugliness, to keep it from overwhelming them.

"It's beating for you," I answer, holding her close. "Only for you."

I turn to Camille to tell her to call the police, but she's already on the phone, speaking fast, pacing back and forth as she talks to a dispatcher. I look down and find her shoes bloody.

Nora looks up at me, her eyes cloudy, distant, removed.

"You stand on a wall to protect what is yours." Her words are simple.

I nod. "You're mine."

She closes her eyes and rests in my arms.

When the paramedics arrive, I refuse to let her go and carry her out to the ambulance myself.

Chapter Thirty

Nora

I'm afraid to wake up. I'm afraid that when I do, it will all have been a dream, and that it won't really be over. I won't be free.

But I open my eyes, and find Brand by my hospital bed.

He smiles, which is the most beautiful thing I've ever seen.

"Hey," he says huskily, in a voice devoid of sleep. "Welcome back."

I look down to find my hand in his, and I look at the clock to find that I've been sleeping for almost twenty-four hours.

I blink, confused.

"The doctors gave you a sedative," Brand explains, seeing the questions in my eyes. "You've been through a lot and you needed a chance to rest before you processed it."

"You've been here the whole time," I say it as a statement, not as a question. Because I already know. I've felt him here all along.

He nods. "Yeah."

I look at him. "You saved me."

It was real.

He narrows his eyes. "You were all set to try and save yourself. The gun... Jesus, Nora."

He closes his eyes for a second, then re-opens them. "Why didn't you tell me? Why didn't you trust me?"

I shake my head, clutching his hand. "It wasn't about trusting you. It was about... being humiliated and entrapped and helpless. I can't explain to you what it feels like to think that my own uncle and father... made me... I was too dirty for you, Brand. Too tainted. You couldn't be with someone like me."

I can't go on and Brand squeezes my hand, lifting my chin to make me look at him.

"*You are not dirty.* Or used. You were forced. You didn't have a choice. But now they won't have a choice either. They're going to prison. They can never hurt you again. And that wasn't your father. Or your uncle."

It's like he knows. He knows that it makes such a difference. Yes, I was still raped. But at least I wasn't raped by my own blood.

"Who am I?" I ask him softly, staring into his blue, blue eyes. "If I'm not a Greene, who am I?"

He shakes his head. "I don't know. Your mom will be back up here shortly, she just left for some coffee. She has all the answers, Nora. But I can tell you this. It doesn't matter to me who you are. Because I already know. You're beautiful and smart and brave. And I love you. I love all of you, no matter what your last name is."

I suck in a breath and the tears start to fall, streaking hotly down my face, dripping onto my hospital gown.

"I love you too," I choke, pressing my face into him, squeezing my eyes closed.

This can't be real.

This can't be.

But it is.

Brand Killien loves me.

He strokes my back, his hands running over my shoulder blade. He pulls my face up into his hands and looks into my eyes. "You will not sink, Nora," he tells me firmly. "You've been tossed by the waves, but you will not sink. No matter what."

My tattoo. *Fluctuat nec Mergitur.* He looked up the meaning. I smile through my tears and nod.

I won't sink. I won't.

"Ma belle fille," my mother says softly from the doorway. I look up, but Brand doesn't let go. I stay clutched to his chest because there's no place I'd rather be. I won't sink because Brand is my anchor. He holds me steady.

"Can you explain?" I ask simply. My mother nods, setting down her coffee and easing herself into the chair by the edge of the bed.

"It's very simple, really," she says sadly. "Your father...Maxwell, I mean, has been twisted for a very long time. He and William... they're an unnatural, hateful pair. I realized it soon after we were married. But I was from France, you see. And after your brother was born, Maxwell knew that he had me no matter what. I knew what he and William were doing together... but I couldn't stop it and I couldn't leave, because Maxwell threatened to divorce me, have me extradited and then he'd keep Nate from me. It was... torturous."

A tear slips down her delicate cheek and even though I should be furious at her for keeping all of this from me, I can't bring myself to that. She's suffered, too.

"Why didn't you tell me?"

My mother drops her eyes. "Because as long as you were a minor, you were trapped with your father. If he had me extradited, you'd have been alone with him. I couldn't allow that. And if I told you, I was afraid that you'd play that hand in an effort to get away from him. And he'd never have allowed that without a fight. Not after grooming you for so long to be a Greene. I was too afraid of what he would do."

"Who is my father?" I ask simply.

She looks up, and she smiles a watery smile.

"Can you not guess? Did you really never suspect?"

I close my eyes and race through my childhood memories and one face comes up in them more often than any other.

Strong hands lifting me onto my horse, strong arms carrying me through the gardens, sharing his lunch, twinkling blue eyes that greeted me every day... and always the warmth. He was always happy to see me, always happy to be near me.

"Julian," I breathe.

Brand cocks his head, questioning.

"Our gardener," I remind him quickly. "But he's more than a gardener. He took care of our house, our horses, me..."

I turn to my mother. "But how... and... I just don't understand."

My mother smiles.

"Julian is from home," she tells me. "You already knew he was French too. I loved him when I was young, but then I was wild and carefree and came to America for adventure. That's when I met and married Maxwell... he needed a normal family to cover up his twisted side. I didn't know that, though, at first. We weren't long into our marriage when I discovered what he was. But I was trapped. And Julian came to save me. I couldn't leave... I couldn't leave Nate. So Julian stayed with me. Always with me. And then of course, you were born, and he had even more to stay for."

Her voice drifts off and she stares out the window, lost in her memories.

"But you... you can leave now," I point out.

She nods. "I can. I can do anything I'd like... because Maxwell will go to prison. I've already called my attorney.

I'll be divorcing him immediately. All will be well, Nora. Finally."

I feel Brand staring at me, and I look up, into the ocean blue eyes that I love.

All will be well.

Chapter Thirty-One

Nora

I cling to Brand, my arms wrapped around his strong waist as we fly down the highway that hugs the lake, on the back of his grandfather's Triumph.

The wind whips my hair behind me and carries the scent of the lake, of the water and the sun, of Brand. And there's no place I'd rather be.

"You ready to stop for lunch?" Brand calls back to me.

"Sure," I answer in his ear.

He pulls to the side, to the little lookout I'd brought him to so many weeks ago, back when he was still limping, back before he was really mine.

We crawl off the bike, take off our helmets, and he digs out sandwiches from a pouch on the back.

As we eat at the picnic table, I prop my legs on his lap and he stares at me thoughtfully, the corners of his eyes turning up.

"Tell me again what you said to Maxwell yesterday," he tells me. "When he called you from the jail and asked you to show leniency, to intervene on his behalf with the prosecutor?"

I inhale, exhale, then smile. Because it had felt really damn good.

"I told him that prison is waiting for him. And that I've heard prison life is hard for pansy-asses like him, so it's a good thing he's a Greene. He can *do what it takes.*"

Brand smiles, a smile full of pride and humor and sadness.

"You're badass," he tells me with pride. "Remind me never, ever to fuck with you."

"Don't you forget it," I answer, putting all thoughts of Maxwell and William Greene out of my head. I'm only focusing on the future now.

"What will you do with your parent's house? I mean, now that everything is over."

He shrugs. "I think I'll just sell the land. I don't want it."

I can understand why. In the weeks since he signed over everything to his mother, she hasn't bothered to contact him.

"What about you?" Brand asks softly, reaching up with a large hand to tuck my windblown hair behind my ear.

"Your mother will get everything at Greene Corp. She said she's going to divide it between you and Nate... you'll be rich, Nora. In your own right. Not working for your father, not under anyone's thumb. You can do anything you want."

I nod slowly, staring out at the lake. "I know. It's a crazy feeling. For as long as I remember, I've been told what I want: to grow up, be a good Greene and head up the legal team for the company. But now, I can figure out what *I* want to do. I can use my degree, or use Maxwell's money to get another degree so that I can do something I actually want to do. Or we can travel the world. The possibilities are endless."

I turn back to look at him and he stares down at me, his expression thoughtful.

I focus on the cleft in his chin. That lovely, adorable, sexy cleft. I reach up and place my thumb in it, where it fits perfectly.

"We fit," I tell him. He rolls his eyes and captures my hand in his.

"In more ways than one," he answers. I blush at that connotation, when I remember how well he'd fit inside of me last night, as we'd rocked together, over and over and over.

We fit.

"I'm sorry I wasn't there when you looked in the box," I tell him suddenly, because the guilt comes back again. It's been two weeks, and I still feel awful that I left him, that I made him feel *not good enough*, when he's better than anyone I know.

He shrugs. "It's ok. I'm ok. Really."

I reach into the pocket of his jacket, where I know I'll find the lock. He's been keeping it there for weeks. I pull it out and stare at it, as I turn it over and over in my hands.

"I'm glad he finally admitted his own guilt," I say simply. "You deserve that."

Brand shrugs again, his eyes guarded as he looks out across the water. "I think I can honestly finally say that I don't care. I *am* free. I'll always miss my sister, but her death wasn't my fault. I know that now."

"I'm glad you see that," I tell him. And I mean it. I'm so freaking glad. I know what it's like to carry guilt for something you can't control. I don't want that for Brand.

I snuggle into his side, absorbing his warmth, soaking him in.

"Tell me about her."

"About Alison?"

I nod.

"Well, she was only four. But she was bubbly and happy all the time. She followed me everywhere. And being the six year-old boy that I was, I'm sure I wasn't always the most patient with her, but I did love her. I'll always miss the sister she would've become and I'll always wonder who she would've been."

My belly tightens, because of all of it... because Alison deserved to grow up and because Brand deserved to have a sister who was his best friend, someone to talk to about girls and confide in and torment and tease.

He didn't get that.

But he did get me. It's not the same, I know. But I'll be his best friend, and his confidante, and I'll never leave him again.

Brand takes the lock from my hands and stands up. He gazes out at the lake, and I see where he's staring. From here, there is a perfect view of the buoy, the fucking weathered buoy that has taunted him most of his life.

With perfectly strong steps, Brand strides down the path to the beach, stopping when his toes hit the water. With one quick movement, he hurls the lock out over the lake. With laser precision, it hits the bell on the buoy before it bounces into the water and immediately sinks below the surface.

For a moment, the sound of the bell echoes down the beach, haunting and eerie.

Brand climbs the hill and stands in front of me, a strange grin on his face.

"I rang the fucking bell."

I smile and shake my head.

"Yeah, you did."

And all of a sudden, the air around us is lighter and I know why.

Because it's gone.

All of it... the guilt, the hate, the bitterness... all of it is gone.

I press myself into Brand's arms, enjoying the way they wrap around me and hold me close, the way all is right in the world when I'm here, the way he loves me.

The way he's mine.

I stand on a wall to protect what is mine.

I'm his and he's mine.

It's the way it's meant to be.

We'll protect each other forever, for the rest of our lives.

No matter what.

***

Brand

Nora and I ride the old Triumph for hours, and I enjoy everything about it. I enjoy knowing that my grandpa had once ridden this very bike. I enjoy the way Nora wraps herself around me, trusting me to keep her safe. I enjoy the wind and the sun and the sky that is so vast and huge and everywhere.

We ride for hours until we finally ride home, to Gabe's little cottage. As we get ready for bed, I look at Nora.

She stands in front of the window, bathed in the silvery light of the moon, and I know that she's everything I'll ever want. She's more than I ever knew I deserved and then some.

She's beautiful.

And she's mine.

Looking up, she catches me looking at her and smiles. "What?"

I shake my head as I turn back the covers of the bed. "Nothing."

We climb into bed, tumbling into each other's arms, the way we have for weeks, as if turning to each other in the dark will keep all of the ugliness away. Because you know what?

It does. It really does.

Nora strokes my face, letting her fingers slide down my cheek, until her fingertip presses into the cleft on my chin.

We fit, Brand.

"We've got to get back to reality," she tells me regretfully. "I've got to get to know Julian as my father. You've got to figure out what to do with your parents' house, then we've got to decide where to live."

I stare at her in the dark.

"We should probably decide where to live first, before we do anything else."

She smirks. "Smart ass. Fine. Where do you want to live?"

I'm quiet for a minute as I ponder that and for the life of me, I don't care.

"I don't care where we live," I tell her honestly. "I just want you with me. We can live in California by the ocean, we can live in the countryside in France, we can live in the city in Chicago or New York... it doesn't matter. I just want you with me."

Nora stares up at me, her full lip quivering.

"Agreed," she answers softly. "You're home to me, Brand."

A lump forms in my throat, and I try to swallow around it, as I think of every fucking thing that has happened over the past couple of years.

"It's funny how things work out," I muse aloud. "Two years ago, I thought my world was ending, that nothing would be ok again. But everything happens for a reason. All of those twisted paths in my life led me to where I'm meant to be.... which is right here."

"With me," Nora sighs happily, squirming closer.

"Yeah," I agree. "With you."

"Before we fall, we fly, Brand," she reminds me softly, tracing the tattoo on my forearm. "Your gran was right."

"She was right about a lot of things," I answer, as I flip her over and hover above her. Nora raises an eyebrow.

"Such as?"

"Well, you've got to take life by the balls and shake it as hard as you can."

She giggles and leans up to kiss my neck. "Your gran said that?"

I nod. "Yeah. You'd like her."

"We need to go visit."

"Yeah," I agree. "We do. She'd like you, too."

"What else was she right about?"

I stare into Nora's eyes, long and hard. "Well, she was right about one other thing. The best things in life are worth fighting for."

Nora sighs a shaky sigh and puts her head against my chest, closing her eyes.

After a minute, she opens them again.

"I can still hear your heart."

I smile in the night.

"I should hope so. It's yours."

Nora grabs my face and pulls it to hers, kissing me as soundly as I've ever been kissed, soft then hard, then harder.

Her hand trails over my chest, over my hips, down to where I'm hard for her.

"Make me yours, Brand," she breathes.

I smile.

"Gladly."

Epilogue

One Year Later

Brand

Gabe meets us at the door of the nursing home, his face drawn and grim.

"Dude, I'm sorry we had to call you home from your honeymoon. We all knew it was coming, but..."

I shake my head and clasp his hand tightly.

"It's okay. I would've been pissed if you hadn't called."

Nora walks beside me, her slender hand on my back. When we'd gotten the call, she hadn't even hesitated, she'd just started packing our bags.

"We have to go, Brand," she'd said.

I've never loved her more.

We flew nonstop through the night, and when we landed, we found out, with relief, that we weren't too late. Gran was still holding on.

"She's waiting to talk to you," Gabe tells me as we walk down the halls. It smells like medicine here. And Ben Gay. And quilts.

I nod. "It doesn't surprise me. Gran has always done things her way. She'll die her way, too."

"Hell yeah, she will," Gabe agrees.

I'm surprised at the knot that is still in my throat. I haven't been able to swallow it, not since we got the call and jumped on the plane. The very idea that the world is going to lose such an amazing person is sobering.

I take a deep breath as I face her closed door, as I stare at her nameplate.

Helen Vincent.

There's no use putting it off. It won't change a thing. She's going to die whether I'm at her side, or not.

But I need to be there, like she's been for me all of these years.

We step into her room and find Jacey sitting next to the bed, holding Gran's wrinkled hand. Gran's eyes are closed, but when she hears my voice, she opens them and smiles tiredly up at me.

"It took you long enough," she complains good-naturedly and everyone laughs. They laugh through their tears because it's very, very evident that this strong woman has grown weak. Her body is limp, her smile is tired.

It won't be long.

A chill runs down my spine as I sit on the bed and pick up the hand that Jacey had just put down. Gran has been well loved. I know that. And I know its time. She's ready to rest.

"You know me," I finally answer. "I'm always running late."

"Not for long," Gran tells me, her little hand squeezing mine. "You've got a wife now to keep you in line."

She closes her eyes again, and I watch the rise and fall of her chest beneath the sheets. She's so small, so frail. It's hard to believe that I once thought of her as big. She's child-sized now.

Jacey catches my gaze from across the room.

It won't be long, she mouths. I nod. I know. Jacey looks as tired as Gabe, as though they haven't slept in days.

Behind her, Dominic sleeps in the chair by the window, here to share this moment with Jacey, to support her. Just like Nora is here for me.

Everything is how it should be.

"Where's Maddy?" I ask Gabe. He nods his head toward the door.

"She took Eli outside to run some energy off. She'll be back shortly."

Gran opens her eyes at that. "That boy looks just like you, Gabriel," she croaks. "He'll be twice as ornery, too, if God believes in payback."

Gabe smiles and holds a cup of water to her mouth, pushing the straw between her lips.

Gran stares up at me. "Can you believe this? They treat me like an invalid here."

Everyone laughs and she takes the cup in her own hands, taking a sip. She hands it back, then settles into the blankets, folding her hands on her chest.

"I did so want to see everyone," she murmurs. My chest tightens and I pat her hands, not quite sure what to do.

"I wanted to see your face before I went to sleep, Branden," she continues. "You're as much mine as these two are."

My chest tightens even more.

I bend down and brush a kiss across her forehead. She smells like lavender and sunshine, the way she always has.

"You're mine, too," I tell her, my voice cracking. "Gran, I want to say thank you... for everything. For always taking care of me, for all of the advice... for giving me a home."

She smiles now, again, without opening her eyes.

"Nora is your home now," she tells me softly, so softly I have to bend to hear her. "You're flying, Branden. You're finally flying."

I literally have to turn away, to steel myself so that I don't sob like a baby right here in front of God and everyone. But I glance up and find that Gabe's eyes are watery too, and Jacey is crying softly as well.

All of a sudden, though, Gran's eyes fly open and she stares at a spot on the wall, above our heads, as intent and rapt as she can be.

"Olen!" she exclaims, and she reaches out her arms. "Wait for me. Don't leave." I stare in shock as she smiles at someone we can't see, a sigh escaping from her lips, as though she's finally somewhere she desperately wants to be.

As though she's finally home.

And then, then... she turns to me, her eyes glazed and happy and distant.

"Your sister is there, Branden. I see her. She's safe and sound. Don't you worry, I'll take care of her for you."

Then, without pageantry or fanfare, the wisest and kindest woman the world has ever known closes her eyes.

I watch her chest shudder to a stop, and I know she'll never open her eyes again.

She's gone.

The world seems frozen as I drop my head into my hands and cry with abandon. I hear the sobs of everyone else, then Nora's hands are on my back, and Gabe's voice breaks through my sorrow.

"Brand?"

I look up at him, my eyes red and hot.

"I never told Gran about your sister."

The entire room is completely still, absolutely frozen, as they wait for my answer.

"Neither did I."

Nora gasps and her eyes meet mine, and a strange peace suddenly filters down around me, like a blanket.

Like a shield.

I smile and pull my wife close. Looking out the window, I find that the sun is breaking through the clouds, shining for all the world like the angels are singing, welcoming Gran home.

All is well.

The End

Acknowledgements

I have the best team on the planet. Words aren't enough to thank them. I will just have to hope that they already know how much I appreciate them. But in a feeble attempt:

My agent, Catherine Drayton, is wise, fierce, classy and amazing.

My publicist, K.P. Simmon is fiery, sharp, loyal and a true dynamo.

My critique partner and best friend, Michelle Leighton, is holy-amazeballs-awesome...in every way.

I need to thank these three ladies for putting up with me, for holding my hand when I need it, and kicking me in the pants when I need that, too. Thank you.

I also need to thank Shannon Briggs, a high school classmate who is now a physical therapist. She was integral in making sure that Brand's injury and treatment were plausible and realistic. Thank you, Shannon, for answering all of my questions and being so patient with me.

Thank you, as always, to my family for putting up with me during the writing process. Living with a writer isn't the easiest thing... we're always dreaming, always staring off into space, always inserting ourselves into lives that aren't our own. There are times my family eats a bunch of take-out, times they put up with watching me wear the same clothes for three days straight and days that

I forget to wash my hair. Thank you for loving me anyway.

Thank you to the special ladies who have chosen to get #BRANDed. You are each amazing: Jennifer Poole, Lori Smith, Katie Anderson, Alyssa Matthews, AnnaMarie Mondro, Eleanor Noach, Nayab Haych, Momo Xiong, Jenn Bernando, Neda Amini, Fran Owen, Danielle LeFave, Margay Justice, Kristy Louise, Melissa Arthur, Danielle Schaaf, Chelsea Cochran, Jennifer Harried, Lana K, Ashley Amsbaugh, Monica Pulliam, Rosemarie McKenzie, Valerie Fink, Jammie Cook, Jennifer Poole, Jacquelyn Lane, Jocelyn Roberts, Roxy Kade, and Fern Curry. Thank you for everything you've done, ladies. You're amazing.

Thank you to the awesome bloggers that read my work and share it. Word of mouth is the best way of spreading the news about a book. I am honored that you take the time out of your days to read my work, and I'm humbled that you love it enough to share it. Thank you.Thank you to my readers. You are amazing, and you are the sole reasons that I get to do what I do. Thank you for loving my stories and my characters. Thank you.

Author's Note

In addition to everyone I mentioned in the Acknowledgements, I need to thank two people who are no longer here to hear it: My grandparents.

Their names are Olen and Helen. I used them in the book as my small tribute to them. They were the wisest, kindest, most amazing two people I've ever had the honor of knowing. My grandfather was wise and strong and loyal- and he served in the Army back during WWII. My Grandma was wise and strong and amazing...while the boys were at war, she went into the Cessna plant and built airplanes for them. She told me once, a good riveter could talk, chew gum and spit rivets at the same time.

They taught me many, many wise things. There are too many to share them all, but here are a few:

Money doesn't buy happiness. It's very, very true. Money brings different sets of problems. Happiness comes from finding it yourself—within yourself, within your own family, within your own life. If you aren't happy, change that. You're the only one who can. Be strong, be healthy, and happiness will follow.

Don't go to bed angry. And if you are still angry, at least say goodnight to each other....so that you both still know that you're still 'in it together'. They were married for a long time, in the happiest marriage I've ever seen. I have to believe they knew what they were talking about.

No one is better than you. Someone might have a more important job than you, but no one is better. My grandpa shared that with me once, and I've never forgotten it. It's how I was raised, and it's how I try and treat everyone now. I'm not better than anyone else, and no one is better than me.

This too shall pass, honey. This was one of my grandma's favorites. I must've heard this a thousand times when I was younger. When something bad would happen and I was beside myself with worry, she'd pat my hand and say, "This too will pass, honey. It always does." And you know what? She was right. It always does. Today always turns into tomorrow and the problems eventually fade away.

This series has always been about overcoming challenges. There will always be a challenge to face, sometimes small, sometimes large. But it's those flaws in life that make it interesting. It's those flaws that heal to make us stronger.

Knowing that, don't be afraid to live life. Don't be afraid to fail, don't be afraid to go at it full steam ahead. If you fail, that's okay. Get back up and try again.
Be strong, be fierce. Love yourself, love others, and allow them to love you back.

Love is the most important thing, more valuable, more powerful and more resilient than any other thing in the world. It will get you through things that nothing else will.

I said it in IF YOU STAY, and I'll say it again…the most important thing that my grandparents taught me: Love never fails.

Count on it.

About The Author

Courtney Cole is a novelist who now resides in Florida after deciding that the North was just too freaking cold. She still loves Lake Michigan, although now she substitutes the ocean for days at the beach.

To learn more about her, please visit her blog, www.courtneycolewrites.com or her website, www.courtneycoleauthor.com

CPSIA information can be obtained at www.ICGtesting.com
Printed in the USA
LVOW07s2031150715

446355LV00008B/904/P